Hurting You

A BLACKTHORN ELITE NOVEL

USA Today Bestselling Author

J. L. BECK
C. HALLMAN

1

STELLA

Pushing the trash down one last time, I pull up the sides of the bag and make a knot with the plastic flaps. I can't believe I almost forgot this one. Paul would have had a mental breakdown in the morning if I had left the trash in here.

It takes pretty much all the strength I have to lift the full bag out of the bin, so instead of carrying the sucker out, I decide to drag the heavy thing behind me. Hopefully, it won't leave scratches on the university's pristine cafeteria floors. I need this job too badly to get in trouble for something stupid.

It's eerie here without all the students. The huge space is so quiet and empty, but yet, I prefer it over seeing all the rich kids walking around inside. I try really hard not to be jealous, but it's not that easy. All-day long I have to look at these people who have everything I've ever wanted. A family, an education, and a chance at a good life. And the worst part is that they don't even seem to appreciate what they have.

I've lost count of how many times I've overheard someone here complaining about the most ridiculous things. Being upset about a store being out of the newest designer shoes or handbags. Not getting the special edition sports car that they wanted. Having to wait an extra day to get their hands on the newest iPhone... the list goes on. Every complaint more absurd than the next.

Meanwhile, I'm working my ass off just to make ends meet. With my parents gone and my grandma suffering from dementia, all the responsibility for my grandma falls onto me. With that, comes a stack of bills every month and that is the reason I didn't go to college, even though I had the grades and the ambition to go. Instead, I took any job I could get right after I got out of high school just so I could support Grams and myself.

When I finally make it to the back door of the cafeteria, my arms are sore from dragging this heavy-ass bag. What the hell do they throw in here? *Concrete blocks?* I push open the heavy metal door and step out into the crisp evening air.

It's dark outside, and the wind is cold as it whips against my skin, but I enjoy the freshness of it after being stuck inside all day. Reaching the dumpster, I try to figure out how to get this overstuffed trash bag lifted into it without breaking my back. Grunting, I lift it with all my might, but barely get it off the ground. Damn thing.

A sound from behind me has me jumping out of my skin, and I gasp quietly. It's probably just a raccoon or something. With my heart jackhammering in my chest, I sneak a peek around the dumpster to check, but there's nothing...

Another sound, this one sounding more like a grunt, which is definitely not a raccoon, causes my curiosity to pique. I should have remembered the saying; *curiosity killed the cat...*

Leaving the trash sitting on the ground, I tiptoe around the dumpster to peek around the corner of the building. I know I shouldn't be sneaking around, but this is literally the most exciting thing that's happened to me in weeks.

Except it's not quite excitement that I feel when I look around the corner. It's more like dread and fear. The blood in my veins turns to ice, and the air in my lungs stills at the sight before me. Two guys are lifting a third guy into the trunk of a car.

My head conjures up all kinds of explanations. The guy is drunk... just passed out. It's probably a prank... no way did I walk in on a murder.

One of the guys shuts the trunk and turns to his friend, asking leisurely, "Where are we going to dump his body?"

A loud gasp leaves my lips before I can stop it from coming out. My hand flies to my mouth to cover it, but it's too late. Both men turn to me, staring at me as I stand there, probably realizing that I just witnessed what they did.

A beat passes, then another, and we just stare at each other. My body is petrified with fear as I take in the two guys before me. They're both tall, looming above me by at least a foot, and muscular like athletes. They're also well-dressed, leading me to believe that they're some rich kids. I'm positive I've seen them before, and I am one-hundred percent sure they go to school here. Even with the dim lighting above, I can tell that one of them is blond with piercing green eyes, the other one is brown-haired with dark eyes.

Without realizing it, I get lost in those dark brown eyes, their depth sucking me in, letting me momentarily forget where I am and what I'm doing.

"Stay here, I'll take care of this one," brown-eyed guy states to his friend, and suddenly, I snap out of it. The trance he has on me is broken, and just when I thought I couldn't get any more scared, he lunges for me. His long legs taking huge strides toward me. *Shit.* As if my brain is finally catching up with my body, knowing damn well if I don't start moving, I'll become just like that guy in the trunk, I unfreeze.

Without thought, I turn and bolt. I don't know where I'm going, all I know is that I need to get away. My feet pound against the pavement, and my lungs burn as I force my legs to push me harder than they ever have before. I wish the ground would swallow me whole and take me away from this place and the guy who is about to *take care of me.*

Refusing to look back, I sprint through the dark night, hoping and praying that I'm fast enough to get away. Hoping for my life, and for my grandma's life, that I can survive tonight.

2

CAMERON

Fucking shit! No one was supposed to be here. How did we not hear her coming? Like a mouse, she remained hidden watching us for god knows how long. Forcing my legs to go faster, I chase after the chick who just witnessed us throwing James' dead body in Easton's trunk.

Though her face was hidden in the shadows, I know she is young from the way she runs, the way her long silky blonde hair falls behind her, and the way her ass moves with every stride. I'll bet she has a pretty face too, and soft lips.

Too bad I have to kill her now.

My dad might be the chief of police, but there is only so much he can do to keep me out of jail. I have to take care of this one myself, and that means I can't leave a witness. I'll have to make her disappear.

With each second, I close in on her. She might be fast, but I'm faster and stronger. Before I know it, I'm catching up with her. I can hear her breathing, each gasp entering her lungs. Once I'm directly behind her, I reach out my fingers circling her slim arm, pulling her backward, and into my chest. Like a banshee, she lets out the loudest shriek possible, so loud that, for a moment, my ears start to ring.

Struggling, she tries to pull away, but I just tighten my grip and fling her onto the grassy area beside us. Before she can get up, I climb on top of her, straddling her torso. Using my arm, I push my elbow to her throat and slap my free hand over her mouth.

I have to give it to her, she is a fighter, like a bucking bronco she struggles beneath me. Her nails rake out and cut across my arms, shoulders, and neck. She's fighting as if I'm about to kill her. Then again, I guess that's why I chased her down. She's a tiny little thing, short, with not much meat on her bones.

Her nails sink deep into my forearm, and I let out a hiss between my teeth. Before she can do any real damage, I release her throat, and gather up her arms, tucking them between our bodies. Lowering myself onto her body, I immobilize her completely. For some reason, I get a thrill out of it. My cock hardens to steel in my jeans, and a rush of euphoric pleasure fills my veins.

With my face mere inches from hers, I brush some blonde strands of hair that are stuck to her clammy forehead away. She smells like fear, but beneath that, I catch a hint of vanilla, and something sweet. Like a curtain being pulled back, I get my first real good look at her.

Focusing my attention on her face, I stare blankly at her. Her eyes are wide, fear and terror pooling within them, while big fat tears fall from the corners. Even scared shitless, she is beautiful, absolutely stunning. I can't quite make out the color of her eyes in the dim light, which only adds further to her appeal.

She is like a mystery to me. Pandora's box. There is something about her, and I can't quite put my finger on it. But whatever it is, it intrigues me. Dreadfully, I'm reminded that I won't be able to explore my interest in her. Turns out we met at the wrong place, and the wrong time, and now I need to get rid of her, not figure her out.

"Don't worry, I'll make it quick. No pain," I try to soothe her, but my words only frighten her more. Her lips quiver under my hand,

and her whole body shakes, tremors of fear own her. She tries to say something, but her words are nothing more than a low mumble with my hand placed over her mouth.

My own heart hammers in my chest. It isn't like I do this all the time. Hurt people, chase girls down, and snap their necks, and had it not been for her seeing what we did, I wouldn't even think about doing this.

"You want to say something?" She nods as much as she can within my hold. "Are you going to scream if I take my hand away? Because if so, I'm going to have to hurt you." Who am I kidding? I'm going to have to hurt her anyway.

Shaking her head frantically, she pleads with me with nothing more than her eyes, and because I'm a glutton for punishment, I slowly lift my hand.

Truthfully, I'm not sure why I do it, maybe because I want to hear her voice and see if it's as beautiful as her face, or maybe because I want to give her a chance to speak her peace. Either way, I remove my hand, setting myself up for failure.

As soon as her full lips come into view, she starts talking. "Please, don't kill me. I swear, I won't say a word to anybody. I really didn't see anything. Please...please, please. I take care of my grandma, and she doesn't have anyone else. Please," she begs for her life, and all I can do is watch her swollen lips move while she talks. So pretty, so kissable. I want to taste them. I don't understand why I'm so taken with her.

"What's your name?" I ask her even though I shouldn't. I shouldn't let her talk either. I shouldn't even look at her. All of this is going to make it ten times harder to kill her.

"S-Stella," she tells me through trembling lips.

Stella...

"W-what's y-your name?" she stutters, her eyes darting around, and I can't help but smile at her effort to be brave.

"I probably shouldn't tell you that, sweetheart."

Hope blooms in her eyes, "Does that mean you're not gonna kill me?"

"I don't know yet," I say, only then realizing that indeed I am unsure if I can kill her anymore. Surely Stella will squeal, and I couldn't blame her if she did. If I were in her shoes, I'd be pissing myself. Imagining my hands wrapping around her slender neck and squeezing the life out of her has my stomach-churning. Can I kill an innocent? I just watched James die, and I feel no remorse, but he was a disgrace to humanity, so I probably did the world a favor by letting him go. She, on the other hand, is a different story.

Then again, what is the alternative? Easton and I going to jail for the rest of our lives? Can I spare her life and endanger ours? Could I harm her just to keep my ass out of prison and my family name out of the gutter?

I don't know...

Rolling off her, I move to a standing position and pull her up with me. I doubt she's going to walk back with me to Easton. In one swoop, I pick her up and throw her over my shoulder. She weighs hardly anything, which only adds to the guilt of hurting her. How can I kill some innocent girl, who is half my size and weight?

"What... what are you doing?" she asks, her voice frantic. Her hands slap against my back before she starts fisting the material of my sweater.

"I guess we're gonna take a vote on if you'll live or die," I say as I carry her back to the car. To my surprise, she goes limp. I half expected her to be scratching my back, kicking her legs out, and maybe screaming. But instead, her limp body hangs over my shoulder as she lets me carry her like a sack of potatoes. I don't even think she is crying anymore.

Has she given up? As soon as I walk around the corner and Easton comes into view, he gives me a questionable look.

"Did you kill her?" he asks once we're within earshot.

"Not yet." At my words, I can feel Stella's grip on my sweater tightening. Okay, so she still has a little fight in her.

"I'm going to be sick," her strained voice meets my ears. "Please let me down. I think I need to throw up."

Not wanting her to puke all over me, I place her back down on her feet. As soon as I do, she tries to get away, but I keep an iron grip on her wrist.

"Don't even think about it," I growl.

She takes a few steps before doubling over, vomit pouring from her mouth and all over the ground. I keep hold of one arm, pulled back, while she uses her free hand to steady herself on the side of the dumpster.

Easton walks up to us, his gaze sweeping over her from head to toe. I know immediately what he is thinking because it's the same thing I'm thinking. Bent over like this, her perky ass is pushed out, and it's hard to ignore how perfectly shaped it is. Round and yet firm.

He gathers her long blonde hair and pulls it back to keep it out of her face while she's puking her guts out. After she empties the entire contents of her stomach, or what seems to be all of it, and is done heaving, she slowly straightens back up.

Using the sleeve of her shirt, she wipes her watering eyes and mouth.

Easton releases her hair, and I watch the silky strands fan out over her shoulders. Then he pats her on the back, and with a low chuckle, says, "Good job, sweetheart. Puking just saved your life."

Raising an eyebrow, I look at my friend. Before I can ask him what the hell he's talking about, he grabs her other arm and starts pulling her toward the car. I let go of her and let him take over. Obviously, he has some kind of plan I don't know about yet.

"What are you doing?" she asks when they reach the car.

"Give me your hands," Easton orders. She hesitates but holds out her hands after a moment. I watch curiously as Easton grabs both and pulls them to the trunk of the car, making her touch the metal around the lock. With a grin, he says, "Now your fingerprints are on the car, and you've left your DNA at the scene of the crime."

"I... I didn't. I wouldn't tell anyone..." Her eyes are wide and frantic as she looks between the two of us.

"This ensures our safety and yours. We go down, so do you, and believe me when I say this..." Easton leans into her face, and even I can feel the darkness in his voice, "If you try and pin this on us. If you tell the police any of this, we won't just kill you. We'll do way worse. By the time we're done with you, you'll wish you were dead."

Easton's threat hangs heavy in the air, and looking at Stella's expression, I think she is trying to figure out if he is serious or just trying to scare her. Soon she'll realize that he means everything he just said.

People at Blackthorn know Easton as the pretty boy who gets more ass than a toilet seat, who has good grades and likes to spend his free time at the local strip club getting lap dances. But there is a darker side to him too. A side that most people don't know or have ever seen. He's vicious and cruel when he needs to be, and if our lives are on the line, then he'll do whatever he can to protect us.

"What were you even doing back here anyway?" I ask curiously. She looks to be our age, but I know she doesn't go to school here. I would've definitely noticed her way before now if she did.

"I-I work here. In the cafeteria." She nervously bites at her lip. I wonder what she's thinking, aside from the fact that we're crazy and she's scared.

"I guess we'll see you around then," Easton smiles like we just met up for lunch and are now saying our goodbyes.

Stella seems unsure of what to do. "So, you're letting me go?" Surprise coats each of her words.

Easton cocks his head to the side, "Unless you think we are making a mistake by letting you walk away?"

She shakes her head, "No, no! I won't say a word. I swear!"

"Good. I doubt anyone would believe you anyway. I mean, it

would be the word of two students against the word of a poor girl," I tell her. I don't know why I said it like that, but as soon as the words leave my mouth, I regret being so condescending. Her eyebrows draw together, and her lips form a tight thin line like she's offended by what I said. I shouldn't care, but somehow, I do. Shoving those feelings down from where they came from, I wave her away.

"Off you go then," dismissing her like a parent does their child. She stares at me for a moment before taking a hesitant step back. She's watching me as if she thinks I'm going to pounce on her any second now. "It's not a trick, you can go," I assure her.

She gives Easton and me one last look, before turning around and running back inside. I watch the door close behind her, wondering if we just made the biggest mistake of our lives. If she says anything, we can kiss our future goodbye, but if she doesn't, maybe we could... *No*, I don't even want to think about it. I can't have her and won't have her.

3

STELLA

*D*riving home, I feel as if I'm losing my mind. Even in a moving car, I find I'm looking everywhere, waiting for something to jump out and get me.

Not something. Someone.

"Stop being paranoid," I mumble to myself. They let me go, surely, they won't seek me out again, so long as I keep their secret, which shouldn't be a problem since I'm not planning to say anything to anybody. Not only did I leave my DNA and fingerprints all over the place, but like blond guy pointed out so eloquently, it's the word of two rich guys against mine. These two probably have an army of lawyers behind them, while I have, well... nothing.

So, you tell me, who is going to believe anything I say? *No one, that's who.*

I take a little longer getting home, driving around aimlessly just in case someone might be following me. I'm terrified out of my mind, but there isn't anything I can do. After a short while, I feel secure enough to go home, and a few minutes later, I drive up to my grandma's simple one-bedroom house, which is essentially my house too since I've lived here for the last sixteen years of my life. Putting my old piece of shit car in park, I take one more deep breath before opening the door and getting out. I cannot have a mental breakdown in front of my grandma.

I can't. As soon as I open the front door, my nose wrinkles; the smell is pungent and hangs in the air like a heavy fog. Something is burning, and even though I've just stepped inside the door, I can see the smoke wafting from the kitchen. *Not again.*

I don't know if it's because I've already spent my amount of panics for the day or because this isn't the first time this has happened, but for some reason, I don't freak out. I just walk into the kitchen and take the smoking pan off the stove.

"Grams?" I call for her, but she doesn't answer. I'm not worried though. She's always here, somewhere. I turn off the hot plate and open the kitchen window to air the smoke out. Then I head for her bedroom.

Cracking open the door, I find her lying in her bed, peacefully asleep. Sneaking into her room, I take a seat on the edge of the mattress. Her eyes open almost immediately. A sleepy smile tugs up her lips.

"Hey, pumpkin, I just laid down for a nap while you were in school," she explains. I don't correct her, and I don't tell her about leaving the stove on before taking a nap, because she doesn't remember anyway. And she probably won't remember this tomorrow either.

"How was your math test? Did you get a good grade?"

"I'm not going to school anymore, remember? I graduated."

"Oh, you did? When is the graduation party?" she asks, her voice pitched with excitement. The party was months ago, and she was there, but again she doesn't remember, which hurts my heart.

"It's soon, Grams... soon." I rub her arm, wishing I could fix her broken mind. "I'm going to make us something to eat, okay? Come out when you're ready." I give her a soft smile, which she returns, and I leave the room.

The sadness I always feel when seeing her like this surrounds me. It's so strong that I almost forget what happened to me earlier today. *Almost.* How did my life get so fucked up? Why can't something go right for once? I cook, and clean, and talk to Grams until she falls asleep again, but nothing eases my mind.

My body is so tired, exhausted, and all I want to do is go to sleep, but my mind is going at a million miles per hour. I can't seem to shut it off, to find peace, even for a second. I'm wide awake, with no chance of sleep in sight, so I do the only thing I can.

I toss and turn on the pullout couch. I've been sleeping in the living room for a while now. There is only one bedroom, and it used to be mine, but with Gram's state of mind and me getting up early for work, I let her take the room. I don't mind sleeping on the couch, yes, it's not the most comfortable thing, but I'd rather it be me than Grams.

I try to calm my mind, but every time I close my eyes, I see them... and I don't know if I'll ever get them out of my head again.

∼

THE SUN RISES, shining brightly through the windows, but I'm in no way, shape, or form ready to get up. Probably because I haven't slept yet. The worry inside of me is eating me alive, threatening to swallow me whole. I don't know how I'm going to make it through the day. All I can think about is last night. Those two boys, the dead body, whatever they were doing, and the fact that I have to go back to Blackthorn for work.

But I think the possibility of seeing them again is what worries me most. It's not like I can just quit my job and go somewhere else. The pay is good, and it's close to home, but I don't know that I can stomach seeing them again.

Ugh, maybe I can manage to find another job on one of my days off, but for right now, I need to get ready for the day and drag my butt to my current one.

By the time I leave the house, my grandma is still sleeping. I made her breakfast and left a note on the table; hopefully, she'll find it and won't try to burn the house down again. She's been doing good lately, but the risk is there every day. Someday she's going to do something, and I won't be here to stop her.

Hurrying to the car because it's still freaking cold outside and my sweater jacket doesn't do much to protect me from the harsh morning air, I get in and start the engine, I blast the heat, turning it to high before pulling out of the driveway. Now that it's light outside, I feel a little less paranoid but not much.

As I drive to work, I'm consumed with fear. Who were those guys? What were they doing with that body? Did they really kill that other person? I have a thousand questions that won't ever get answered because no way in hell I'm going to ask them, and the option of going to the police is completely out of the question.

If I'm going to survive this, I'm going to have to force myself to forget what happened.

The closer I get to Blackthorn, the more my fear consumes me. When I pull up to the employee parking lot, my heart is beating so fast, my chest is hurting. I've got to get my shit together before I walk in there. Otherwise, everyone will know that I'm losing it, and something is up.

Checking the time, I realize that I'll be late if I sit here any longer, so I take a deep calming breath and get out of the car. For every other step I take, I look over my shoulder once. Scanning the area for one of the two guys. Expecting them to jump out from behind a car and around every corner I see.

I purposely take the side door instead of the back alley. No way I'm going back there unless I absolutely have to.

"You left the trash bag on the ground outside," Paul, the kitchen manager yells at me, as soon as I step inside. The sound of his voice startles me, and I clutch a hand to my chest to keep my heart from springing out of it.

"What?" I gasp, trying to hide my fear.

Paul's gaze drifts down to my chest, where my hand clutches my shirt, and, for a moment, I feel weirdly exposed. I know he is not looking at my hand, but my boobs. I hate when he looks at me like this, it gives me the creeps.

Finally, he raises his eyes, for a moment, I see the lust flicker in them before his gaze turns stern. "I said you left the trash bag outside on the ground."

Oh shit. With everything that happened last night, I completely forgot about the trash. "I'm sorry, it was too heavy, I couldn't lift it into the dumpster." It's not a lie, but I still feel bad for letting him down.

"Some critters got into it. There is trash all over the back alley. You need to go and clean it up before you clock in."

"But... I need my full pay..."

"Either that or we need to come to a different arrangement," he says, licking his lips. I almost throw up right then. What an asshole. I'm not sure what arrangement he is talking about, but I'm sure that I don't want to know either.

"I'll clean it up before clocking in." I force a smile, but it hurts to make my lips go that way. The one place I wanted to avoid is the one place I now have to go back to, but that is still better than staying here with Paul.

Grabbing some gloves and some smaller trash bags from the storage room, I go out back. I half expect the two guys to be there, waiting for me, but they aren't, and their car is gone. *Thankfully.* The alley looks different in the light, but it still gives me the creeps.

As quickly as I can, I clean up the mess and deposit all the trash in the dumpster, trying not to look at my dried-up vomit that's next to it. When I come back in, I toss the gloves in the trash and wash my hands, wishing I could wash the memories swirling in my head away too. Paul is already hard at work, and so I start in on my duties for the day right away.

Before it gets busy and most of the students come in for breakfast, I quickly refill the condiments, cutlery, and napkins. I carry a box of everything, so I don't have to make multiple trips. When everything is full and organized neatly, I put the remaining stuff back in the box and turn to leave.

I'm just about to disappear into the storage room when a couple of students cut in front of me, one of them slamming their shoulder into me, knocking the box out of my hands and onto the ground. I watch in horror as a stack of napkins, and about a hundred straws go flying across the floor in every direction.

"Oops, sorry," the guy mumbles but doesn't even stop to offer to help pick up the mess be caused. Cursing under my breath, I drop to my knees and start picking up the stuff, tossing it into the box with an angry vengeance.

"Here, let me help you," a female voice pierces my ears, and before I can look up, a girl appears next to me. Crouching on the hard ground to help me pick up what I dropped, she mutters with a frown, "What a jerk, right?"

"Oh, it's okay. You don't have to help me. This is my job." I tell her.

The last thing I need is to be reported for ruining some Blackthorn royals lunch. I need this job; my livelihood depends upon it.

"It's not your job to deal with meatheads like him though," she jokes, and for the first time today, I smile. While I'm picking up the napkins, I peek over at the beautiful girl helping me. It doesn't take much for me to know that she is definitely a student here. Manicured nails, a designer handbag hanging off her arm and, perfectly curled black ringlets of hair that makes her appear as if she just got back from a high-end salon.

She looks like the typical Blackthorn student, rich, beautiful, and successful. Everything about her screams high class. The only thing that is different is that she actually stopped to help me, instead of walking by like she was better than me.

"Willow..." Some guy calls out from behind us, getting our attention. I look up to find the mystery guy standing at the door, holding it open with one hand. There is a darkness in his eyes, and he watches me like a frog might watch a fly as it flies around its head. "We're going to be late for class."

"Oh crap, I got to go," the girl tells me and dumps what she had picked up into the box.

"Thank you!" I call after her before she grabs onto the guy's hand and gives him a kiss on the cheek. I watch her, and the guy who is obviously her boyfriend, disappear, the door falling shut behind them. Stupidly, I let my mind run rampant with thoughts and wonder briefly if she knows how lucky she is to have all the things she has. Hurrying, I pick up the rest of the stuff and tell myself to stop thinking of a life I will never have.

I spend the rest of the day washing dishes, peeling potatoes, cutting onions, and carrots. Usually, I wait to get the trash until everyone is gone, but today I don't. I go around the cafeteria and empty out every last trash bin, gathering them all by the door, so I only have to go outside once. Part of me wants to ask Paul to do it, but I know better. It's my job, so I'll suck it up and do it. It's not like it's dark out yet.

Grabbing the bags, which, by the way, feel like they weigh more than me, I shove through the back door. I look both ways and hurry over to the trash can. I start to toss the bags into the dumpster, the sound of shoes crunching against the asphalt pierces my ears. Like a crazed woman, I whirl around, one of the bags of garbage still in my hands.

Lord, please help me. It's the two guys from last night. They're standing near the only entrance into the building. My only exit. Have they finally come to kill me? Tears well in my eyes. They have, they've decided that I can't keep my mouth shut.

4

EASTON

"*I* ... I didn't tell anyone," is the first thing that comes out of her pretty little mouth. Big pale eyes and golden blonde hair that curls at the ends give her an angelic look. I remember how soft it felt in my hands last night, and I have the urge to touch it again.

I can't take my eyes off of her. We've been on the lookout for her all day. I barely slept last night, wondering if we made the right choice. And I'm not talking about killing James, that was no doubt the best choice for everyone. The guy was a total creep and a number of other things. No, I'm talking about letting that blonde-haired angel go. If she talks, we are in some seriously deep shit.

And that's exactly why we're here right now. We need to make sure she keeps her pretty little lips sealed.

"We figured you wouldn't tell anyone, because you're a good girl. Aren't you, Stella?" I ask her, loving the way her name rolls off my tongue. I can see her squirm from where I'm standing. Cam and I agreed on taunting her a little, making sure she stays in line. Fear is a powerful motivator, and as long as she's afraid, she'll do whatever we tell her to do.

"Yes, I won't say anything. I swear!" she squeaks and drops the bag in her hand in the process. She doesn't make a move to grab it, and I enjoy the sight of her frozen, struck with fear.

Would she look at me like that if I touched her right now, or would she melt beneath my fingers? Every time I thought about her today, it stirred something up inside me, and it's not just fear of her going to the cops. There is something about her, something that draws me in, something I want. My interest in her is strange, foreign but intriguing, and quickly turning into an obsession. Something I can't stop thinking about, something I need to have and can't let go.

What the fuck are you thinking, idiot?

"We still wanted to swing by and remind you," Cam tells her, pulling me from my stupid induced thinking.

"You don't have to remind me, I won't forget," she says, her voice hesitant like she's not sure if she was supposed to speak at all.

"I mean, there are other ways we can keep you quiet... you can't talk with a dick in your mouth." Her gaze widens, almost as if she didn't expect me to go there. "We could fuck you if that's what it takes, fuck you into silence. You are pretty, and I'm always looking for something new to sink my dick in to."

"N-nnooo..." She shakes her head, her golden hair flying everywhere. "I won't tell a soul, you don't have to... to do that." I almost bust out in laughter at the red in her cheeks. Is she embarrassed talking about sex? Wait, maybe she's a virgin...that would be the icing on this cake.

"You sure?" Cam licks his lips and gives her a smoldering look. He is, after all, the smooth talker. Asshole has chicks coming on his dick every night. Of course, I can't complain myself.

Stella nods, "I won't say anything, just please, don't hurt me."

"It would only hurt a little. Mostly it would feel good... really good," I promise her. "But we understand. We'll let you get back to work then, just don't forget to keep your mouth shut. Otherwise, we'll find something to fill it with."

I dismiss her like she's nothing to me. Cameron and I both take a step away from the door, giving her a walkway to go back inside.

She nods, her eyes darting between the two of us like she is trying to see who is going to attack first. When we don't move, she starts walking toward us. I can see her knees shaking from here, but she doesn't stop once. When she passes us, she's so close that I can smell her shampoo and perfume or whatever that heavenly scent is. It makes my mouth water, and I'm tempted to reach out for her and tug her into my chest.

Her steps are small and slow, up until she is past us, then she scurries to the door like she's suddenly in a hurry. She pulls the heavy metal door open, but before she can step foot inside, someone screams from the kitchen.

"Stella!" At the sound of her name, she jumps, her shoulders tense, and a small shriek escapes her lips. "Where the hell are you?" The male voice continues. Hearing the condescending tone he is using, makes me want to go inside and cut off his fingers and shove them down his throat. I know I have no reason to be protective of this girl, after all, she holds our lives in her hands, but I am.

"I'm coming!" she yells back.

"And you better put the damn trash bag inside the dumpster this time." The same voice booms through the door and into the alley. I don't know what it is about him yelling at her, but it really rubs me the wrong way. If he keeps it up, he's going to be brushing his teeth through his asshole. Stella twists her head around, looking over her shoulder at us. Her gaze then moves and falls to the floor where the trash bag is sitting. She doesn't make a move to get it, which means she is more afraid of us than the guy she is working for. *Good.* I'm satisfied with that.

Crossing my arms over my chest, I stare at her, a tiny grin on my lips.

Come here, baby...

Cam being the knight he is, leisurely strolls over there, picks up the bag and tosses it into the dumpster. When he turns back around, the bastard winks at her, and I can't help but grin wider. This is going to be so much fucking fun.

She actually mutters, "thanks," before turning back around and disappearing inside. The door shuts behind her, and I turn to Cameron.

"That went well," he grins.

"It did, but I think we need to make certain she understands just how far we are willing to go. I want to make sure she truly believes us."

"Yeah?" Cam cocks his head, "What you have in mind?"

"I think we follow her home and give her a little taste of what we can do to her."

I can see the wheels in Cam's head spinning, "I'm pretty sure she's a virgin, given her reaction to what you said earlier, and I'm not okay with taking her cherry tonight."

I give him a deadpan look, "I didn't say we were fucking her. I highly doubt she would allow that to happen. I mean testing the waters. Let's just mess with her a little bit, corner her, maybe get a little taste of her. Find out if she really is a virgin or not."

Normally, I wouldn't have to try for a girl, they come to me, on their backs or knees willingly, but Stella is a whole other beast. She's going to fight us tooth and nail, but she'll enjoy it. I'll make sure of it.

"Yeah, let's do it. She intrigues me. Not really sure why. She seems to be the simplest girl here at Blackthorn, and yet she's not simple at all."

"I get it." And I do because in my own mind I'm trying to rationalize the growing obsessive thoughts I'm having about her. I want to know everything there is to know. "Can you get information on her? How old, address, and stuff? Find out anything we can use against her?"

Cam rolls his eyes, "Do you think this is my first rodeo?"

"No, but it's the first girl you've ever had to learn the name of," I tease.

"Shut up. When you're fucking them, they all look and sound the same. Plus, names aren't needed when I'm giving them the best orgasm of their lives."

Cam's a playboy and an asshole. I'm just an asshole with a dark obsession that I hide well. It's no secret that we both like to share, and Stella, she might just become our newest conquest.

"Tonight, we show her what we're capable of."

"Tonight," Cam says, and we walk our separate ways.

FOLLOWING Stella home was easier than I expected. For a girl as terrified as she is, she lead us right to her house without a single pitfall. Granted, even if she was looking for a car following her, she wouldn't have seen us through the thick black cloud of exhaust her car drags behind her. She needs a new car, like yesterday.

We follow her into the shittiest neighborhood in town and watch her pull into the driveway of a small rundown house. Jesus, the girl, has charity case written all over her. It's no wonder she works at the school instead of attending it.

She barely has two pennies to rub together.

As a safety measure, we park a good block away and watch her get out of the car and walk into the house. I don't like the fact that she's so oblivious to her surroundings. She should be paying better attention. Watching her back. There are a lot of assholes out there that could hurt her. *Assholes like us...*

"This neighborhood is terrible." Cam points out the obvious.

We wait in the car for thirty minutes before we get out and walk down the sidewalk.

"Should we break in or just ring the doorbell?" I ask, not being sarcastic at all.

"Let's surprise her," Cam snickers, and we make our way around the house. We walk up to the back door, and I can already see it's not going to take much to force our way in. There is a thin looking glass in the center of the door that will be easily broken.

Before we even get close to the door, a floodlight above us switches on, shining a bright light on us. *Shit.* I look at Cam, who just shrugs his shoulders at me. A moment later, the same door we were about to break down opens, and a gray-haired lady appears in front of us. Fuck, this wasn't part of the plan. I'm about to spout out some random excuse of why we are creeping around at the back of her house when she surprises me by smiling widely.

"Oh, there you are," she greets us like she was expecting us to be here. "Well, come on in, don't be standing out here in the cold." Stepping aside, she opens the door wider to make room for us.

Okay... This is odd. I give Cam a questionable look, but he doesn't miss a beat, taking the invitation, and stepping inside. Shaking my head, I follow him.

The backdoor leads straight into the kitchen. It's small, the furniture is colorful and mismatched, but it also has a strange kind of cozy appeal to it.

"Why don't you go make yourself comfortable in the living room, and I'll whip you up something to eat since you just missed dinner?"

"Grams? Who are you talking to?" Stella's voice comes from somewhere in the back of the house. "For the love of God, do not turn on the stove, Grams!" There's a panic to her voice.

Her grandma suddenly looks distraught as if she just remembered something bad. She opens her mouth to talk but is interrupted by Stella's loud shriek. All heads turn toward the door where Stella just appeared. She has a flimsy towel wrapped around her, but besides that, she is standing naked just a few feet away from us. Her hair is still wet and sticking to her slender neck and shoulders. Drops of water catch in the light against her porcelain skin.

"W-what are you doing here?" she asks, her voice as frantic as the clutch she has on the towel. "Grams, come here. Step away from them," she tells her grandmother nervously.

"What's wrong?" Her grandma asks the same panic in her voice now.

Shit, this is getting out of control.

"Nothing is wrong," I try to defuse the situation. "We were just coming by to say hi."

Stella looks between us, panic like I haven't seen before in her eyes. I'm pretty sure she is more scared right now for her grandma's life than she was yesterday for her own.

"Grams, it's late. Why don't we get you ready for bed? Come on, I'll help you." Stella talks to her grandma like she is a child, and suddenly it clicks. She's her caregiver. Grams must have Alzheimer's or dementia or something like that.

"Yeah, Grams, why don't you go get some rest," Cameron coos. Gently, he takes the old woman's arm and leads her across the room to where Stella is standing. Then he leans in and whispers something into Stella's ear. She stiffens but nods before leading her grandma away.

Walking over to him, I nudge his side, "What did you tell her?"

"I told her she better not dare put clothes back on," he smirks. "Now, let's get comfortable in the living room," he walks away and toward the multicolored couch.

I can already feel my cock growing to life, "Yes... let's."

5
STELLA

Oh, god. They're here, in my house... with my grandma. No, this can't be real. I can handle being scared for myself but not for her. Now they have something to use against me. Grams gets into bed without complaint, and like a child, I tuck her in.

Briefly, I entertain the thought of calling the cops, but then I remember where I am. I don't even know if the cops would show up in this neighborhood anymore and if they do, what would they do? Would they help me? Would they believe me? Shaking my head in defeat, I decide to not risk calling the law.

I really want to put on a shirt and a pair of sweatpants before going back out there, but his instructions were clear, and I don't want to tempt them into hurting me.

Quietly, I close Grams' bedroom door. With a death-grip on the towel, I walk back to the living room on shaky legs. Half-naked, and with my wet hair sticking to my skin, I'm freezing. My whole body trembling from a combination of fear and cold. I try to take a calming breath, but I can't seem to get enough air to my lungs. I'm so light-headed I think I might seriously pass out.

When I enter the living room, I find the two guys sprawled out on the couch like they own the place. My heart starts to beat out of control as I imagine what is going to happen next. I don't know what they are going to do to me, but my imagination is running wild. Whatever it is, I need to stay quiet because I can't let my grandma get hurt. I'll do anything to protect her.

"Don't look so scared," the blond one, who reminds me of a jock, says, "your Grams is going to be fine... It's you we want." He grins, but I feel anything but a smile coming on. I feel sick taking in the two men sitting on my couch, the place I sleep. The two of them couldn't look any more out of place here.

They are all put together, wearing new expensive-looking clothes, their hair is styled, and their shoes are shined. Everything about this house is old, scuffed up, and falling apart.

"You look cold," the other one points out. "Why don't you come here, and I'll warm you up?" I shake my head, but still, find my feet moving all on their own.

"W-what do you want? I told you I wouldn't tell anyone, and I haven't. Isn't that... isn't that proof enough?" I stop at the edge of the couch, and the brown-haired one reaches out for me. I clutch onto the towel a little harder when his finger touches the edge of it.

"Sometimes the proof is in the pudding, wouldn't you agree, Cam?"

Huh? What does that even mean?

"I would agree..." The guy named Cam smiles, but it's not a cheery smile. No, this one is cruel and promises dark things. Things I know I'm not going to be ready for.

"Which means we need to see how well you can follow directions. We need to make sure you'll listen to us when we tell you to do something," the blond one says this time, and my gaze ping pongs between the two of them.

"It's time for your first test, Stella." Cam pulls at the edge of the towel, and because I'm so caught up in the back and forth, my grip has slackened. In an instant, the towel is pulled away, and I'm left completely exposed to these two immoral men. Letting out a squeak, I use my hands to cover my breasts and vagina, but there's no point. They've already seen me.

Both men's pupils dilate, and their nostrils flare as if they've just taken a whiff of a porterhouse steak being brought to them. I take a hesitant step back, considering the option of running, but with Grams here, there isn't anywhere for me to go. Where could I go with her in the next room, and myself completely naked?

Nowhere, that's where, and they know it. Like a wounded and trapped animal, my eyes dart around the room.

"Don't even think about running or screaming. Grams is in the other room, and believe me when I tell you, you don't want to wake her. You don't want her to see what we have planned for you." My bottom lip starts to quiver, fear encasing my body in a block of ice.

"Come on now, be a good girl and sit down on my lap," Cam uses a soft voice that sounds like it's been dipped in honey. Sexy and drawn out. Any other woman might be hypnotized by that sound, but it brings me nothing but pure terror.

Gathering all my courage, I force my limbs to move. Turning around, I lower myself onto his lap. His hands find my hips, and he pulls me back, steadying me until my bare ass makes contact with his jean-clad thighs. Immediately, I feel his hard length pressed up against my backside. I try and block out the terror I'm feeling. I'll do anything they want so long as they don't hurt Grams.

My back is straight and stiff as a board, while my face is turned away from them. Somehow not seeing them is even worse. Not knowing what they are going to do next has me on a cliff's edge and scared out of my mind. I can't tell you how fast my heart is beating, just that it's trying to escape my chest. I can't breathe or think.

A warm hand gently touches between my shoulder blades, and I damn near jump off Cam's lap at the touch. All he does is run it down my spine, caressing my skin softly. It should be a calming touch, but he might as well be dragging a knife across the flesh. Dread and worry consume me, leaving me exhausted and cold. I fold my arms across my chest, trying to get warm.

"What do you think, Easton, can we get her to relax a little?" Cam speaks to his friend. At least they finally revealed their names to me. It's only a tidbit of information, but it makes them seem a little more human now that I know their names.

"Yeah, I think I know something that might loosen her up," he chuckles. "Lean back, sweetheart. Let us take care of you."

Take care of me?

Before I can think too much on it, Cam tugs me back at my shoulders, until my back is flat against his chest. I want to recoil, be disgusted by him, but my freezing skin appreciates the warmth he is offering, and without thought, I cuddle deeper into his chest, my arms fall to my side.

He doesn't seem to mind, his hands snaking around my body to cup my breasts. He gives them a light squeeze, sending small jolts of pleasure straight to my core. Taking my nipples between his fingers, he rolls the hardening buds lightly.

I've never been with a man before, let alone two, and while fear is rooted deep inside of me, there is a curious warmth blooming in my center. It's confusing because I know deep down, I shouldn't want this, but somehow, I do.

"Have you ever been touched like this before?" Easton questions gingerly.

"No," I answer, hoarsely. His eyes light with either excitement or fascination, which I don't know. It was probably stupid of me to answer that question, but I'm too afraid to lie and too smart to provoke them.

"Perfect." Easton reaches for me, his fingers gently slide up my leg. His touch is warm, but it paralyzes me with fear. When he reaches my knees, I consider locking my legs together. But there are two of them and one of me. It won't take but a second for them to overpower me. I'm helpless, completely at their mercy.

"Relax, Stella. Let us make this good for you..." My knees knock together, and I bite the inside of my cheek.

"Please," I whimper as he pushes my legs apart, my pussy coming into view. My legs end up on either side of Cam's thighs, and he uses that leverage to spread me open even wider. Easton pauses, his eyes lifting from my center and up to my face.

"We make the rules, sweetheart, and we need to know that you can follow those rules."

"I can," I muster up a response. Cam shifts his hands, keeping one on my breast while moving the other up to my neck.

"Good, then sit back and show me that you can," Easton murmurs. I want to continue watching him, but I'm left gasping when Cam's fingers circle my throat, squeezing my flesh tenderly.

"I can't wait to listen as you fall apart on his hand, your tight cunt gushing your sweet release." His filthy words shouldn't have an effect on me, other than disgust, but they do. They make the burning ache deep inside of me, roar to life. With my head forced back and Cam's hand wrapped around my throat, I'm forced to rely on feeling alone.

The softest of gasps passes my lips as Easton's fingers make contact with my pussy. He traces my folds, up and down, making leisurely strokes that have me panting after a few seconds. I don't want to give in to the feelings I'm having right now, but I can't escape them either.

"So fucking pretty and pink. Soon, I'll need to taste you, sink deep inside you. You want that, don't you?"

All I can do is whimper as Cam starts to roll my nipple between his fingers, causing flames of pleasure to lick at my skin. I let my head fall all the way back against his shoulder, our faces so close together. Everything about this is so intimate. I'm completely naked, and they are so close, so close they are all around me. Invading all the space.

Easton easily finds my clit and starts to rub circles against it, giving me just enough friction to crave something deeper. My hips lift out of instinct as if my body knows what it needs, and how to get it.

"Such a greedy pussy." Easton pulls away and then shocks me when he lands a hard slap against my pussy. I gasp, a spark of pleasure pulsing deep inside of me. It threatens to consume me if I let it and I want to, so fucking badly.

"Oh, god..." I mewl into the air.

Cam chuckles behind me, the sound vibrating through me. Before I can gather my wits, Easton's doing it again. This time the slap is a little harder, and my clit throbs at the assault.

"You like that, don't you?" Cam whispers into my ear, his lips pressed against my lobe.

I swallow thickly, feeling the gush of arousal in my pussy. Before I can respond, Easton is on me. He does it again, and again, each slap a little harder than the last, but still landing with an effectiveness that is astounding. My face burns and my body aches with a need that I can't alleviate.

"Please, please," I beg, my core tightening. I've never needed a release so much in my life. My body feels like a coil, tightening more and more.

"Tell him what you need," Cam encourages. His hand squeezing my throat, but never enough to freak me out or to make it hard to breathe.

"I..." My chest rises and falls rapidly, but it barely feels like I'm breathing. "I... make me..." I'm ashamed to even say it or be asking for them to make me come. It feels wrong and dirty, and somehow, I know the only way to end this is to let them bring me to the cliff's edge and push me off.

"Say it," Easton growls, his fingers trailing over my pussy, this time closer to my entrance. Yes, that's where I need him, want him.

I grapple for control, wanting a release but not wanting to admit it.

Cam pinches my nipple again, a current of heat ripples through me, zinging like lightning to my core. "Say it, tell him what you need."

The want is consuming me, drowning out the rational side of my mind. All I can think about is finding a way to make the ache go away. And that's through these two men.

Defeated, I answer, "Please, make me come."

The second the words leave my lips, Easton is pushing a thick finger inside of me. There is a sting of pain, but I'm so wet and ready for him that it's easily forgotten after the second thrust. Spreading my legs wider, I let him own me, finger fucking me with a darkness that blankets the goodness that I ooze.

"Fuck, she's tight. Perfect," Easton hisses, but I can't focus on his words. Only the pleasure he's awakening inside of me. Cam sucks at my throat, his teeth sliding across the skin.

"Mhm," I moan, my impending orgasm just on the horizon.

"Soon, sweetheart, soon." Easton's voice holds promise, but I ignore him and focus on nothing more than the unbridled pleasure consuming me. Like lightning rippling across the sky, I start to come, my eyes flutter closed, and my pussy pulses, clenching around his finger.

My back arches as my body contours on its own. I'm vaguely aware of Cam's erection pressing into my butt cheek, but in this moment, I don't care. If they wanted to fuck me all night, I would let them. I would do whatever they want, and not because I'm scared. In this moment, I just want them, want them to make me feel good, to touch me, hold me, fuck me.

Slowly, I start to come down from the biggest orgasm of my life. I'd made myself come before, but nothing ever felt as all-consuming as this. Like a leaf falling from a tree, I gradually come down to earth.

My body is still limp when Cam moves me around on his lap like I'm a doll and stands up. My eyes fly open, and my arms move to stop him, or at least hold onto him, but I'm already lifted up in the air. He cradles my naked body to his chest as the fog of hormones slowly clears out of my brain, and I'm left with the stark reality of my situation.

With my brain returning to its normal, less endorphin swamped state, my thoughts about letting them do what they want are suddenly gone. Fear replaces them yet again. What are they going to do next?

"Where is your bedroom?" Cam growls, looking around like he is searching for another door… one he won't find.

"You're standing in it," I whisper.

"You sleep on the couch?"

"It pulls out," I defend my sleeping arrangements.

"You have fun with that," Cam tells me, right before he drops me back down on the couch. My body bounces once, the old rusty springs underneath squeaking. "Let's go, Easton."

"I think I've changed my mind. I want to fuck her," Easton announces, looking at my body like he is about to devour me.

"Not today," Cam shakes his head. "Come on, I'll take you to the dorm. You can get some pussy there."

"I've already fucked all the girl at the dorms. I want a shiny new toy… and this one looks fun to play with," Easton says like I'm not here at all. Talking about me like I'm a thing.

The entire time they are having a conversation, I'm just lying there on the couch completely nude. I think about covering up, but it's not like they haven't seen me naked yet.

"Not today," Cam repeats, a little more insistent this time. "She's been a good girl for us, so we'll leave her alone for now."

"Fine, let's go then," Easton huffs, before adjusting his pants.

"Goodnight, sweets. We'll see you tomorrow," Cam winks at me. "Lock the door after us, this seems like a bad neighborhood. Wouldn't want someone to break in and take advantage of you."

I don't say anything back, just watch as both turn away from me and walk out the front door like nothing happened.

CAMERON

Like a total creep, I sit in the corner of the cafeteria by myself, nursing a soda. I normally go home in between classes or find some girl to fuck in the dorms, but today all my thoughts are with Stella. The way her naked little body squirmed around on my lap, her ass grinding into my crotch. Her moans as she came all over Easton's fingers. Fuck, that was so hot. I've been with a lot of girls and done a lot of shit, but that simple little act was one I'll never be able to forget.

I know she is somewhere back there in the kitchen; unfortunately, that's where she usually stays. So far, I've only caught sight of her once. She was getting something from behind the counter, and she didn't see me sitting here while she did.

Frustrated, I'm about to call it a day when she appears in the doorway. In her hand, a rag and a small bucket filled with water. She walks over to the table, furthest away from me, and starts cleaning off the table. Her back is turned to me, and she bends slightly, giving me a great view of her ass. The same ass I had naked on my lap last night. My dick stirs in my jeans, and all I can think of is fucking her, worshipping her little body. It would be the perfect way to keep her mouth shut.

I wanted to fuck her last night, and maybe we should have, but I felt weird having her grandma in the next room. When we fuck her, I want to make her scream without worrying her grams is going to burst through the door.

Watching her move to the next table, I'm ready to adjust my pants to accommodate my growing cock. She moves gracefully like a dancer or some shit. The image of her dancing naked in front of me pops into my head, only pumping more blood to my dick. Shit, I gotta stop unless I want to walk out of here with a raging hard-on and blue balls for days.

When she moves on to the next table, she finally looks up and spots me in the corner. Immediately, her face turns ashen. Her eyes scanning the room like she is looking for someone to help her. *Oh, sweetheart, no one can help you.*

There are some other students here, but none of them are paying her any attention, and even if they were, nobody would stand up to Easton or me. Just like Parker and Warren, we're pretty much untouchable at this school. We could, and do get away with everything, which now includes murder. There is no way to hide from us here, no place we can't get to her.

She must come to the same conclusion because a moment later, she resumes wiping down the tables. Her movements are a little less fluent now, her fear noticeable, making her jumpy and tense. Moving from table to table, she continues wiping the tables down. Glancing over to make sure I'm still sitting here and haven't moved.

When she is only two tables away, she stops, staring at the table between us. I can see her pretty head thinking about it. She doesn't want to come any closer, thinking she could just leave. Lifting my finger, I curl it toward me, beckoning her closer. Even from a distance, I can see her swallow hard, her delicate throat working. She stares at my finger like it's going to give her all the answers. Then she closes her eyes, her lips press into a thin line, and she shakes her head at me. *Big mistake, Stella... big mistake.*

When she opens her eyes again, she takes the bucket and rag, spins around and runs off. Well, she tries to at least. Both of us were trapped in our little bubble, neither of us seeing the three girls approaching my table. Stella bumps into the frontrunner of the girl squad, dumping out the entire bucket of dirty water on the floor, which splashes everywhere and spreads outward like an ice cube against hot asphalt.

"Are you fucking kidding me?" The girl that got splashed with most of the water yells. I quickly realize that I know her. Carla, Cerry, Cami, or some shit like that. Like I said before, names don't matter when you're balls deep inside of them, and I don't make it a common thing to remember their names.

"Oh, my god, I'm so sorry," Stella gasp.

"What a fucking clutz," one of the other girls says. "You better pay for her dress, it's ruined now."

I almost roll my eyes, it's fucking water, the same shit you use to wash your clothes, but these bimbos wouldn't know that.

"Like she could ever afford to buy something like that," Cami says, scrolling Stella.

"I'm sorry, I'll pay for the dry cleaning," Stella offers.

"Don't fucking bother, clean up the floor before someone slips and breaks their neck because of your stupidity."

"Yes, I'm sorry," Stella apologizes again before turning away.

Cami looks over to me. "Oh, my god, Cameron. Did you see that?"

"I did," I nod and watch as Cami and her two friends take a seat at my table.

"I'll have my daddy call here and tell the manager what happened. I'm sure he can get her fired."

"Don't you think you're overreacting a little. It's not like she did it on purpose." I can't believe I'm defending her, but of course, I don't want her to get fired either. How are we going to keep an eye on her if she isn't here?

Cami looks shocked that I would even say something like that, but I really don't give a shit what she thinks.

"Anyway, I was looking for you. I know it's been a while since we hung out, but I got invited to this thing. It's like a fundraiser gala..." Cami keeps rambling on, but I drown out her words. Instead, I concentrate on Stella, who has returned with a mop and a bigger bucket now. She reminds me of a princess that doesn't know she is one.

She starts to mop up the floor, and even watching her do that simple task has me enthralled. I imagine what I'm going to do to her next time I get her alone. After all, she needs to be taught a lesson since she didn't listen to my command earlier. All of this is about having her keep her mouth shut and follow our orders.

"So, what do you think?" Cami asks, tapping my arm with her well-manicured finger.

Blinking from my thoughts, I ask, "Think about what?"

Cami's eyes just about blow out of her head. "Are you coming to the gala with me? As my plus one?"

"Listen, Cami—"

"It's Carly," she interrupts me, a hardness to her voice. *Close enough.*

"I don't do dates, or dances, or any of the likes. I mean, I didn't even remember your name. What makes you think I would go out with you?" Carly's cheeks turn bright red, either with embarrassment or anger, or maybe both. Either way, I don't care. I can be a smooth-talker when I need to be, but since I can barely remember her, I know she wasn't a good lay, so no reason to keep her around.

"You're an asshole," she says like that's going to hurt my feelings. "Let's go, girls."

"You got that right," I murmur.

Carly and her crew get up and walk away, but not before one of her goons kicks over Stella's water bucket. The three hyenas giggle and leave. I lean back and watch the whole scene unfold, wishing Stella would grow a spine and hit that chick upside the head with the mop.

Stella tries her best to ignore me while she starts the cleaning progress all over again.

"Stella!" Some guy calls for her, and I'm pretty sure it's the same guy from the other night. She flinches at the sound of her name but still takes her cleaning supplies and heads toward the guy. I watch her scurry behind the register where a heavy-set guy with slicked-back gray hair is waiting for her.

I can't make out what he is saying to her, but he is yelling at her for something. Her head is lowered, and she just stands there, taking it. Doesn't she know how to stand up for herself? And doesn't he know only Easton and I get to mess with her?

My phone vibrates in my pocket, interrupting my thoughts. I fish it out of my pocket and find a message from Parker lit up on the screen.

PARKER: NOT COMING TO CLASS TODAY?

Shit. I'm late for class.

7

STELLA

Opening and closing the cupboards, I realize it's time to go grocery shopping, which is a shame since I don't have much money left over from paying bills this past week. I make a quick list of the absolute essentials and head out the door.

As I'm walking out to my car, there is a woman standing on the sidewalk, stapling something to a nearby light post. She's dressed far nicer than most in this neighborhood, so I know right away that whatever reason she's here isn't good. People like her wouldn't come here unless they have to.

The nameless woman locks eyes with me and walks over to the car carrying a stack of papers in her hand. Her heels clack against the concrete loudly. My eyes dart down to the stack of papers, and the air in my lungs evaporates.

Oh, god.

"Hi, have you seen this man?" The woman asks a crack in her voice as she shoves a flyer into my face. I can barely breathe, and my response to her question lodges in my throat. "Please, have you seen him?"

All I can do is shake my head and unlock my car and climb inside of it.

Before I can shut the door, she continues, "If you see him, please call the police. He is missing. He is a good kid, but he gets into trouble sometimes. Are you sure you haven't seen him?" The hope in this woman's eyes makes me think she must be his mom or sister.

"No, I'm sorry," I say, finally managing to close the door. I start the car and slam it into drive, pulling away from the curb, watching while the woman stares at my taillights in horror as I drive away without helping her.

It doesn't matter though. Even if I did want to tell her, I couldn't. *I wouldn't.* Grams' life, hell, my own depends on my silence, and I can't risk that, so forcing myself to calm down, I push the lady's face from my mind and head to the store. I can't change what's already happened, only where I'm going now.

∼

"CAN you please try one more time? I don't know why it would be declined. I'm sure I still have thirty bucks on this card."

"Ma'am, I already tried four times. It keeps saying the same thing... insufficient funds." She whispers the last thing as if the three people behind me in line didn't already get what's going on.

Looking down at the bags full of groceries I can't buy, it takes a lot not to cry. I really need this stuff, but I'm not about to beg. Nodding to the lady behind the register, I put my useless debit card back in my otherwise empty wallet.

I feel someone's presence behind me before I see his arm come around me. He slides his shiny black credit card in the machine in front of me, and the word *approved* comes up on the screen a moment later. I don't have to turn around to know who it is. He stands so close I can feel his body warmth on my backside, the smell of his cool aftershave surrounds me in seconds. A scent I won't ever be able to forget.

"Awe, thank you," the lady behind the register beams. "That was so nice of you."

"No problem," Cameron's smooth voice meets my ear. He's chocolate dipped in poison. Tempting to the eye, but if you take a bite, it might just kill you.

I'm sure everybody who is seeing this thinks I'm being incredibly rude by not thanking him or even turning around to look at him, but they don't know who he is or what he is capable of.

"What an ungrateful bitch," the guy who has been waiting in line behind me mumbles under his breath.

"Oh, don't worry, she is going to be *very* grateful," Cam responds his voice gravelly, as he places his hand on the back of my neck. His touch is nothing but a reminder of the power he holds over me, of the secret that connects us. A shiver runs through my body as I suck in a shaky breath.

I catch the concerned look the cashier gives me right before she asks, "Are you okay, miss?"

"She's fine," Cameron answers for me, giving the back of my neck a light squeeze. It's a warning. "Isn't that right, Stella?"

"Yes, I'm fine," I murmur as I grab my bags and turn around to face him. His hand falls away then, but he doesn't move his body. Because he is standing so close and the register is right behind me, I have nowhere to go. As always, there is no escaping him.

Since he is much taller than me, I have to tip my head back to look into his eyes. The moment our gazes collide, I wish I hadn't looked at him at all.

The look he gives me sends an icy shiver down my spine. The corners of his mouth twitch as if he's enjoying seeing me scared which only makes me more scared. *Who enjoys instilling fear in others? A crazy person, that's who.*

Finally stepping to the side, he nods his head toward the door, signaling for me to go ahead. I move past him and out the door, refusing to look back at him, though I know he is there, following me like a shadow that refuses to disappear.

Once outside, I feel tempted to turn around and run back into the store. Apparently, I'm not safe anywhere. I make it all of five feet before Cameron has his hand wrapped around my wrist. He walks me to my car but only to put the two grocery bags inside. *Of course, he has other plans.* I shouldn't be surprised. He closes the door and tugs me to what I assume is his car, which happens to be a sleek sports car that looks like it cost more than a year's tuition at Blackthorn.

"Get in," he orders, opening the backseat door for me. I hesitate for about two seconds, but then force myself to move and listen to him, grinding my teeth together the entire time.

I slide into the back of his sleek looking car. The leather feels soft and cool under my fingers, reminding me all over again how, as a rich asshole, he can do whatever he wants. Instead of closing the door behind me like I expect him to, he climbs into the car after me.

"Slide over," he nudges me forward, but I'm already scooting away from him doing whatever I can to put some distance between us. "Not that far," he coaxes, his hand wrapping around my thigh as he settles into his seat. As soon as he closes the door behind us, I feel like I'm suffocating. The space is much too small for both of us.

"I need to go home, my grandma—"

"I can send Easton to go spend some time with Grams while we're busy."

"No!" That would be even worse than Grams on her own.

Cameron just chuckles. "Don't worry, sweetheart. This won't take long. I've been dreaming of your lips wrapped around my cock all day."

My breath hitches at the word cock. Obviously, I've heard it before, but suddenly I feel like I'm twelve hearing some boy say it for the first time. My cheeks heat in embarrassment. I'm half tempted to tell him I've never given a blowjob, but I wonder if that would make things worse.

"B-but...wait..." I start, peering around us. We're inside a car parked at the side of the store, but there still might be people that can walk past us and see inside.

"Windows are tinted, so if you're worried about someone seeing us, rest assured no one will." Cameron reads my mind. But it's not just the fear of being caught, it's not wanting to be in this car with him, trapped and completely at his mercy.

"Why are you doing this? You can get any girl you want, why can't you just leave me alone?" I know mouthing off right now is not my best bet, but at least there is only one of them now, and we are in a semi-public place. If I scream loud enough, someone would help me... *maybe.* Cameron's features turn dark.

"We told you, already. We need to make sure you're going to listen and can follow directions. How else are we going to trust that you'll keep our secret?"

Fed up, I twist around in my seat. I need to reason with him, to figure out what is making them so obsessed with me. If they wanted to kill me, they would. That's not the case though. "You know, I will, so please don't lie to me. Why are you really doing this to me?"

Cameron's lips twitch into a grin. "You're a smart girl, and I suppose you deserve the truth. So here it is. Now, we simply want you, and we always get what we want." He pauses, his eyes scanning my face. Of course, they do. No one can tell them no. "We both want to fuck you. But the best part is that we know we can just take it and there is nothing you can do about it."

There it is. The real reason. Of course, I already knew this. They like the power of it all, they like knowing they can control me and that I'm utterly powerless against them. I'm the prey, and they're the big bad wolves. Now the only question is, am I going to let them control me? Or am I going to fight back?

They'll use whatever they can to keep me in line. I'm their puppet now, and they're my puppet masters. Out of the corner of my eye, I see Cameron unbuttoning his pants and unzipping his zipper, his already erect cock springs free. Like a deer caught in the headlights of a car, the air in my lungs stills, and I take in the smooth mushroom head and the veiny shaft.

"I want your mouth, now," Cam tells me, an edge in his tone I haven't heard before. "Earlier, you didn't listen to me. This is going to be your punishment."

"I was working..." I try to defend myself, but Cameron isn't having it.

"Stop talking," he orders and grabs me by the back of my neck. "Don't worry, I won't hurt you. Now be a good girl and open your mouth."

He tugs me toward him, and because I don't know what else to do, I open my mouth and let him guide me to his cock. He groans loudly when my tongue makes contact with the smooth head of his length. There are about a million butterflies taking flight in my stomach right now, and I don't know yet if they're going to result in a good feeling or bad one.

With his grasp still firm on the back of my neck, he pushes me down, filling my mouth with his length until he hits the back of my throat. I gag at the intrusion, and try and pull away, but he holds me there for a second before he lets me come back up. But my relief is short-lived because as soon as I get a gasp of air into my lungs, he pushes me right back down. His other hand weaving its way into my hair, where he grabs a fist full of the strands.

"Fuck, you feel so good," he growls, his hold on me tightening. He pushes my head down a few more times, making it hard to breathe, but I don't hate it as much as his hand on my neck, where he is squeezing painfully. His other hand tightens, pulling on the thick strands of my hair, making my scalp scream for relief.

Yelping with pain, I try to push away. For a second, I don't think he's going to let me come up, but then he releases his hold on my hair and pulls me up by the neck. I suck in a quick sharp breath; my eyes are watering, and my lungs burn.

"You're hurting me. You said you wouldn't hurt me," I whimper, my voice wrapped up in panic, but I still manage to sit up straight anyway.

"I got carried away," he admits breathlessly, a possessiveness that I'm drawn to appears in his eyes. "And most girls like a little bit of pain."

"I'm not most girls."

"Oh, I've noticed… Now come here and finish what you've started." He releases the hold on my neck and lets his arms fall to the side, giving me an invitation to take control. Deciding that this is better than the alternative, I lower my head again and take him into my mouth. I take my time, running my tongue along the underside, feeling the small slit there. My touch is exploratory, and he seems to like having my hands and mouth on him.

Again, his hand finds its way into my hair, but this time he is gentler, cradling my head instead of grabbing it. His other hand comes around my back, caressing my shoulder as I keep taking his cock deeper and deeper into my mouth on my own.

He grunts in appreciation, the noise vibrating through me, edging me on to take him deeper. I know he's making me do this, and I shouldn't feel turned on or joyful, but some fucked up part of me wants to please him. I want to show him that I can do this on my own. That I can take command and follow directions.

"I hope you're enjoying yourself because Easton won't give up control like this." I want to ask him what he means by that, but that's hard to do with a dick in my mouth. "Yeah, keep doing it, just like that. It feels amazing…" He encourages and my pussy clenches, my own arousal mounting.

I continue sucking him off, letting the world around me fade away. Forgetting why I'm here and why I am doing this. Forgetting that I have no money left for the month. Letting every single worry and fear disappear from my mind and forcing my concentration onto Cameron instead. On his manly scent, on his hands that map out my body. On his huge cock in my mouth.

"Fuck, I'm gonna come..." He groans. "I'm gonna come down your throat. You're going to swallow every drop and prove to me that you can be a good girl."

I nod my head as much as I can. His hands land on the back of my head, holding me still while he thrusts his length into my mouth three more times. I gag as he goes all the way down my throat, but I manage to remain calm, knowing that he is close and that the moment is almost over. Then, with one final thrust, I feel his warm release shoot down my throat.

His whole body tenses, and a loud groan fills the car. When he releases me, I lift my head, his cock sliding out and over my tongue, leaving behind a salty taste.

Sitting up, I move back a hair. With my hands in my lap, I just stare at him, taking in his body. He's breathing heavy, his face and body are relaxed though, and I remember how I felt after they made me come. Like I was a feather floating down from heaven. Cameron's eyes lift to mine, a euphoric fog clouding them. He looks so beautiful, so perfect, and less like the cruel evil monster I know he is.

Lifting his hand, I almost flinch away, but then realize he doesn't intend to hurt me, he just wants to touch me, and so I let him cradle my face in the palm of his hand. Our eyes lock together, and he runs his thumb over my lip, wiping most likely his release away.

"Do you get it now?" he asks, his voice sleepy. "As long as you do as we say, we'll give you pleasure. Fuck up, and don't follow directions, and we will take from you. You do for us; we do for you."

I nod because saying no won't change anything. I'm at their mercy now. The best thing for me to do is do as they say, and hope Grams and I come out of this okay. Eventually, they'll get tired of harassing me, right?

Then I remember what I saw earlier today.

"Someone was hanging up flyers about that guy. You know the guy..."

"Yes, we know. You don't have to worry about that though," Cam brushes it off, but I don't believe him. How can I not worry about that? People are looking for him, people who clearly loved him and I have answers.

"Now, off you go, Grams is waiting." He shoos me away while tucking himself back into his pants. "Oh, and one more thing..." Darkness flickers in his eyes, "Don't you dare go home and make yourself come. Only we get to make you come. Pleasure yourself, and you'll regret it."

"I wasn't going to," I lie.

I was definitely going to, and I still just might.

8

EASTON

"You did what?" I can't believe this fucker.

"Calm down, it was just a blowjob," Cameron tells me like it's not a big deal. We've shared countless times before, but for some reason, the fact that he got his dick sucked by her without me being their speaks of betrayal, which makes zero sense to me because the girl means nothing to either of us.

"*Just a blowjob?*" I almost laugh, "One that I wasn't part of. And after you gave me that big huge speech about her being a good girl and not being ready." I can't believe this fool.

"She wasn't ready that night, not for both of us, plus, she didn't listen to me, which is grounds for punishment to begin with. Also, I'm not gonna fuck her at her grams' place. I'm kinky, but that shit is even too much for me."

"At least tell me how it was, asshole."

"It was... heaven. She is so... innocent." He licks his lips, his eyes unfocused like he is remembering everything. I've never wanted to punch my friend in the face as much as I do right now.

"I'm popping her cherry," I announce, "you got her mouth first, so I get to fuck her cunt first." Maybe that's the better deal anyway. I'll get to make her bleed, feel her slick heat squeeze around me, be the first man to give her an orgasm with a cock.

"Fine, I'll get her ass then," Cam grins. *Fuck, I want that too.*

"I guess," I reluctantly agree because I know I can't have both even though I want both. I'm a greedy fucker when it comes to this girl. I look for her as we sit in the cafeteria, our trays of food sitting in front of us remain untouched. Though the food here is pretty good, I don't often eat it. I usually come into the cafeteria to socialize and pick up girls, but as of recently, to keep an eye on Stella.

"Hey, dude," Parker Rothschild king of Blackthorn greets as he takes a seat in front of us, his girlfriend, Willow in tow. Though he's more Warren's friend then ours, we've all grown a little closer over the last couple of months.

"Hey," Cam replies, while I just give him a head nod.

"What's up?" Parker questions. Willow gives both Cam and I a soft smile as she takes the seat next to him. Sometimes I wonder how an asshole like Parker got a pretty, sweet girl like her. They seem like complete opposites in every way.

"Nothing, what's up with you?" I counter, reaching for my soda, the only thing I've opened on my tray.

Warren takes that moment to walk up and slap my shoulder, almost knocking the soda out of my hand. "Watch it, asshole."

"Well, hello to you too," Warren says, all cheerful as he sits down. Warren, Parker, and Willow break into small talk while Cam and I sit in silence, both watching the kitchen door for any movement.

A few moments later, Harper, Warren's girlfriend, joins the table.

"Hey, babe," he greets her. We all look up and find Harper, who looks to be anything but happy standing beside the table. Matter of fact, she looks like she's in shock as she sits down next to him. "What's going on? Why do you look like you're going to be sick?" he asks, concern etched into his features. Warren doesn't care about anyone, but if I had to guess, I would say he cares about Harper, even if he denies it.

"Did you do it?" she asks.

Warren's face morphs into confusion, "What are you talking about?"

She points to the nearest flyer, and I immediately know what she is talking about. *James.*

"I don't know what that's about. Parker took care of him." Warren looks over to Parker, giving him a hard stare.

"If this is about James going missing, I don't know what the hell happened. I waited until he woke up, and then I told him to go home. He was disoriented and could barely walk but he got up and started walking away." He is only half lying. Yes, James was still alive when Parker left. But he also called us to make sure James got home and kept his mouth shut, which didn't end the way it was supposed to.

"You think you can just rape Warren's girl? Harassing her? Drug her?" Cam punches James in the stomach, and he doubles over. A gargled response passes his lips, but neither of us care about his answer.

Cam's dad has been looking for a reason to jail this fucker forever. Today's his lucky day, I guess. I watch as he tetters on his feet like a skyscraper that's ready to topple over.

"It's time someone taught you a lesson," I growl and flex my hand, opening and closing it before forming a perfect fist. He continues to stumble away from us, but we've already smelt his blood, and like lions cornering a wounded animal, we won't stop until we've had our share.

Pulling my hand back, I punch the bastard in the face one last time. He sways unsteadily, and as if time slows down, I watch him fall backward. My eyes move to the large metal dumpster that he's headed toward, and before I can make a move to stop him, the side of his head cracks against the edge of it.

I know without question, there is no coming back from that. His entire body slumps to the ground, the essence of life leaving his body. I look to Cam, who is just staring at James's unmoving body. Deep down, I know I should feel something, but I don't. I don't feel anything for him, not remorse, not anger, or even fear.

"Are you sure?" Harper whispers so only our table can hear. Her soft voice drags me out of the memory from that night.

Parker leans across the table, "Yes, I'm sure."

"Well, forgive me if I jump to conclusions," she rolls her eyes at him.

"I'm an asshole, sweetheart, but not a killer," Warren whispers into Harper's ear. "Plus, I was with you all night, tending to your hands and knees."

"What happened to him then?" Harper questions once more.

Why can't she just let this go?

"Maybe he got eaten by wolves," I suggest, trying to make light of the situation.

"Doubtful," Warren replies, rubbing at his chin.

"I can have someone check the video surveillance and see what happened after he walked off? But I'm pretty sure the police already took a look at it, so if they didn't find anything, I doubt we will," Parker suggests.

They won't find any video surveillance. Cameron's dad made sure it got destroyed. Perks of being the chief of police.

"Yeah, let's do that. I would still feel better if I knew," Harper says, and I almost shake my head at her. Stupid girl. She shouldn't care about James, not after what he did to her.

"What you mean is, you would rather make sure I'm not lying to you?" Warren snaps.

"I didn't mean it like that," Harper starts to defend herself. I choose to make my opinion known.

"Why do you even care, Harper? I heard what he did to you. Warren told us. If anyone should want him to disappear, it should be you." I pipe up, saying out loud what I was thinking myself.

"I'm just worried. I thought maybe you guys did something, but now that I know you didn't, I wonder if something else happened to him. I know what he did was fucked up, but that doesn't mean we have to be as ruthless as he was."

That's where she is wrong. We need to be more ruthless than the real evil in the world because they are not playing by the rules either, and someone needs to keep them in line.

"If there is anything to be found, the police will find it. No point in worrying over nothing." Parker shrugs, ending the conversation.

Warren, Parker, and their girls sit and talk with us for a little bit longer before they all leave. Cam and I, of course, stay behind until we are the last people in the cafeteria.

"I'm tired of waiting, let's go back there," Cam nudges me in the side, and I couldn't agree more. Patience isn't really my strongest asset, and I've been hungry for Stella all day. Together we get up and head for the door behind the counter.

As soon as we enter the kitchen, we can hear voices carrying through the large space.

"But I need this job," Stella pleads, desperation coating her voice. Immediately my blood starts to boil. The only people she should be pleading with is Cam and me.

"Maybe you should have been better at your job then. You've been fucking up daily, and you've been late multiple times now." An accusing voice meets my ear. It's the same fucker who yelled at her before. Her boss. I clench my hands into tight fists as I walk deeper into the kitchen with Cameron right behind me.

"Please, I've only been late twice, and I made up that time on the same day, and I'm sorry about making all the mistakes and leaving the garbage outside the dumpster. I promise it won't happen again."

We step around the corner, and I spot Stella, who is in the far right corner of the room. The guy she is talking to looms over her, and it takes everything inside of me not to fucking walk right over there and shove him backward.

Since neither of them have noticed us yet, I decide against it.

"That's not going to cut it. I can't keep you here, I mean unless..." the voice trails off. That fucker better not say what I think he is about to say. If he is... I glance over at Cam, who is looking at the scene like he's about to kill someone.

"Unless what? Tell me what I can do. Please, I need this job," Stella begs, and the rage inside me pulses. There is only one thing she should be begging for, and that scenario involves Cameron, me, and her sprawled out naked in my bed.

"You're a pretty girl, you know?" The guy takes another step, closing the distance between them. Stella being the smart girl she is, takes a step back at the same time. He doesn't get the hint though, either that or he doesn't care. "You could get on your knees and suck me off. That might persuade me to let you stay."

Cam tries to take a step forward, but I reach out and grab him by the shoulder, stopping him before he can take another step. Shaking my head at him, I press my lips into a firm line. I want to know her answer. I want to know if she will do it or not. That will determine our next move. From the shadows, we watch the fucker lift his hand and touch the collar of her blouse.

My jaw clenches so tightly I feel my teeth grinding together when he starts to pull it down, exposing a little of her shoulder. I swallow down the anger that's threatening to explode within me. *Say no...* I want her to tell him no, because if she doesn't. If she doesn't, something bad is going to happen, not only to him but to her.

For a moment, Stella just stands there frozen like a deer caught in the headlights of a car. I'm seconds away from sprinting over there, fuck her response. He's not allowed to touch what's ours. Before I can make a move, Stella snaps out of it and slaps his hand away, and then shoves against his chest.

"I wouldn't suck your dick if you offered me a million dollars. You're a disgusting pig." The last word has barely left her mouth, and he pounces on her. One hand circles around her throat, while the other grabs a handful of her blouse, ripping the fabric away from her skin.

I don't know who moves first Cameron or me, a red haze coats my mind. One second we are standing in the doorway, and the next, we are across the room.

My mind goes completely blank... the prick just made the biggest mistake of his life, and he is about to pay dearly for it. You don't fuck with what is mine.

9

STELLA

Paul's meaty fingers dig into the tender flesh of my throat. My chest constricts as he squeezes so hard, I can barely get air into my lungs. Like a wild animal, I lash out, my fingernails dragging across his skin. I do so, hoping that I can cause him some kind of pain to make him loosen his grip, but my actions only seem to anger him more, making him squeeze a little tighter.

Squeezing my eyes shut, I say a silent prayer that I'll make it out of here in one piece. A strange gurgling noise meets my ear, and it takes me a second to realize that the sound came from my throat. I can feel myself growing lightheaded. Just as panic starts to really settle in, Paul releases his hold on me. *Thank god.*

Sagging to the floor, I clutch my throat as I suck in a painful breath. When I pry my eyes open, I don't quite know what to expect, but it sure isn't what I see. Cam and Easton have Paul pinned to the nearby wall. Easton is holding him up, while Cameron is raining down punches on his face. I can hear Paul's head bouncing off the wall with each hit.

"You shouldn't have touched what's ours," Easton growls, the tone of his voice cuts through me like a shard of glass. It's dark and edgy like he's barely holding on by a thread.

"Now you're gonna pay," Cameron seethes between his punches. His voice sounds just as dark and scary as Easton's.

I don't know how I manage, but somehow, I make it back onto my feet. Stumbling through the kitchen, I put as much distance between the three men and myself as I can. I need to get away from here. I can't watch them kill another person. I can't be part of this again.

Without looking back, I run through the building until I make it to the side door. I don't want to draw any attention to myself, so I speed walk to my car instead of running.

I fumble with my keys, my throat aching, and my heart thundering inside my chest but manage to open the door after a few tries. My hands are shaking when I turn the ignition, and the engine roars to life. Hitting the gas, I pull out of the parking spot faster than I should, surprised when I don't hit another car. Tires squeal beneath me as I speed away. Tears prick at my eyes, but I blink them away.

Shit, shit, shit. Why can't just one day go as planned? Am I asking for too much? All I want is to have a normal life. Go to work, go home, take care of Grams, and then do it all over again the next day. Why the hell do I keep ending up in situations like this? My thoughts race through my head, making it hard for me to concentrate on anything in particular.

The drive goes by surprisingly fast, and before I know it, I'm pulling up to Grams' house. I feel a little better now, though I'm still shaking a bit when I get out of the car and walk to the front door. I don't know what's worse, the thought of Paul touching me or the thought of the guys killing him for it. I don't know if I can handle someone dying because of me, even if he does deserve it.

As soon as I open the door and see Grams sitting in the recliner, my heart rate calms, and my hands stop shaking. She looks up at me, smiling while continuing to knit what looks like a scarf.

"Hi, pumpkin, hope you had a great day at school," she greets me cheerfully, completely oblivious of the shitty day that I've had.

"Hi, Grams. I did," I lie, the last thing I want to do right now is upset her. "How was your day?"

"Boring, but I kept myself busy with cleaning and knitting." She looks at me, and her smile suddenly fades, her eyes grow big, and her eyebrows furrow. "What happened to your neck, Stella?"

My hands fly up to my throat, where my skin is already tender. "Oh, nothing." I play it off. "I'm going to take a shower before I start dinner, okay?"

Grams opens her mouth to say something, but I'm already out of the room before she can finish. I speed walk to the bathroom and close the door behind me. As soon as I'm alone again, I sigh and look at my reflection in the mirror. My throat is already red and blue, outlines of each of Paul's fingers decorate the skin. Shit, I'm going to have to cover them up with makeup. I can't return to work like this… who am I kidding? I can't go back to work there, not after what happened.

There are only two ways that things could've ended after I left. One, they killed Paul, which means the cops are going to come knocking on my door very soon, or two, they beat the crap out of him, which means I can't go back because Paul will hate my guts and most likely fire me anyway.

Either scenario leaves me in the center of a shitstorm and without a job, which means I need to find work elsewhere, and I need to do so fast.

All I want to do is cry, but I can't. I have to be strong, not only for me but most importantly, for Grams.

Things could always be worse.

I tell myself as I strip out of my clothing and turn the shower on. Maybe if I go to sleep, I can wake up in the morning and pretend that none of this happened.

Wishful thinking, huh?

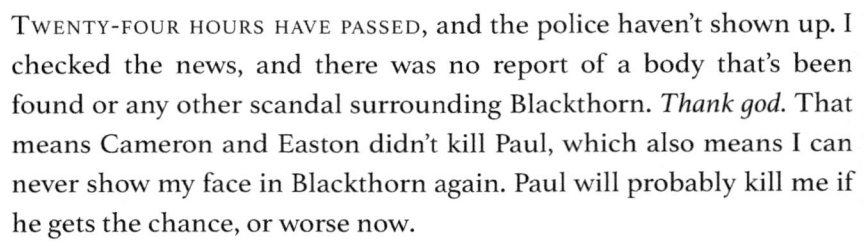

Twenty-four hours have passed, and the police haven't shown up. I checked the news, and there was no report of a body that's been found or any other scandal surrounding Blackthorn. *Thank god.* That means Cameron and Easton didn't kill Paul, which also means I can never show my face in Blackthorn again. Paul will probably kill me if he gets the chance, or worse now.

Maybe not going back there isn't such a bad idea. If I don't go back, maybe Cam and Easton will lose interest in me. *Out of sight, out of mind.* One can only hope.

Rifling through my closet, I find my best-looking outfit, consisting of black slack pants and a light pink blouse, and put them both on. I only have sneakers available, not flats or heels, but hopefully, they won't look down at my feet when I ask for a job. I shake off the nervous feeling in my limbs and force a smile onto my face.

The bell above the door rings as I step into the diner. The hostess, a middle-aged lady with curly red hair, greets me with a wide smile. "Hey, sweetie pie. Coming in to dine with us?"

"Hi, ah... I'm actually here to see if you are hiring right now?"

"Oh, sweets. I'm not sure about that. Let me ask Amanda, our manager. You come and sit in the booth over here, and I'll go get her for you."

"Sure, thank you!" I tell her and take a seat in the booth she pointed to. A few moments later, the hostess returns with a woman in tow, which I'm guessing is Amanda.

"Hi there," she greets, extending out her hand to me. I stand and take her hand, giving it a light shake.

"Hi. I'm sorry to come in unannounced, but I was just wondering if you are hiring?"

"Don't worry about that." She smiles before continuing, "We aren't actively looking, but we usually always need some extra waitresses. What kind of experience do you have?"

"I worked as a nanny for a while, and I used to stock at the local grocery store. My most recent job was in the kitchen as a helping hand at Blackthorn University."

"So, you don't have any experience being a server?"

"No, just more like in the background. I'm not great with people." As soon as the words leave my mouth, I realize that I couldn't have said anything dumber.

Apparently, Amanda thinks the same because she tips her head back and starts laughing.

"I'm sorry," I say, shaking my head.

"Don't be, I appreciate your honesty. However, I can't help you out with a job. I'm looking for people with experience. I'm sorry." She sounds genuinely sorry as she gives me a sad smile.

"It's okay. Thanks for talking to me." That's more than I can say from the last three places I've been.

"You know what. I might not be able to offer you a job, but I can offer you a slice of our famous apple pie. You sit right here and let me get you a piece. I promise it will make you feel better." I doubt it, but I appreciate her kindness.

Amanda gets up before I can object and disappears into the kitchen, leaving me sitting alone with all my problems, each one hanging over my head like a heavy cloud.

"Hey, sorry..." An unfamiliar voice says. I turn my head to see where the voice comes from. Two beautiful girls are sitting in the booth next to me. They both stare at me, their eyes soft. "I overheard that you are looking for a job."

"Ah, yeah. Do you know a place?" I ask, hope blossoming deep inside me.

"Yes, actually. And it makes good money too, at least 2k a week," one of them tells me. She has long blonde hair and big blue eyes rimmed with black eyeliner and long thick eyelashes.

Wait, did she just say two thousand a week? I can barely contain myself. Then again, at the back of my mind, all I can think of is being a whore, or drug dealer, both of which I would not be good at.

"What kind of job?" I ask suspiciously. If it sounds too good to be true, it usually is, and I'm in need of legit work, not some fake shit.

"You ever heard of Night Shift?" The other girl asks. She has dark brown hair and hazel eyes that gleam with mischief. I can tell that she's trouble just from one single look.

Night Shift. The neon letters pop into my head, it's a club not far from my house actually. "Like the strip club?"

"Yes, the strip club," the hazel-eyed girl smirks, "you are very pretty, and you have the girl next door vibe, mixed with something that makes you wholesome. If you're interested, you could make a lot of money."

"I don't know..." *Stripping?* Could I really take my clothes off for money? Even if it is a lot of money? I mean, I am desperate, but am I that desperate?

"No need to decide right now. I'm Valorie, by the way," the brown-haired beauty introduces herself, and then she points to the blonde girl, "This is my friend, Katie."

"Hi, I'm Stella."

"Nice to meet you, Stella," Katie beams. "If you're really looking for work, I would head over to Night Shift. We could even vouch for you. Help you get your foot in the door. And you don't need any experience there."

"Not with a body like yours," Valorie adds. A soft blush starts to form on my cheeks, and my confidence blooms.

"Maybe I'll stop by there," I smile.

Amanda returns with my pie then, and I undo the silverware to dig in, just as my cell phone starts to ring. I internally groan and pull my cell out of my pocket. The number isn't one I recognize, but I decide to answer anyway because I've filled out so many applications; it could be any of them calling for an interview.

"Hello," I try and sound as cheerful as possible.

"Hello, is this Stella Young?" The man on the other end asks, his voice holding authority. Immediately, I'm caught off guard.

"Yes, this is she. Who is this?"

"This is the Jaspen county police. Miss Young, could you tell me where you are right now? I'd like to send someone to talk to you."

"What? Why... I mean, what is this about? Am I in trouble?"

"No, no... nothing like that. I'm afraid I have some bad news..."

10

CAMERON

Panic claws at my insides. *Where the hell is she?* It's been days since we've seen Stella. She didn't show up for work at all, and every time that we've tried to call her phone, it's gone straight to voicemail. Normally, I wouldn't give two fucks about a girl, but Stella isn't just anyone.

I've been wanting to go over to her place, but we had to deal with this Paul mess first. This fucker seriously tried to call the cops on us because we roughed him up a bit, okay, maybe more than a bit. Still, he deserved it. Truthfully, he's lucky I was able to pull Easton off of him because it could've ended way worse.

Of course, my dad smoothed things out, and Easton's mom helped too. It just took them longer than expected. While waiting, we had to lay low, my dad basically put us on house arrest, but that's done with now. Now we're free again.

Easton gets into the passenger seat of my car. He closes the door, and I speed off, heading toward Stella's house. I cut the twenty-minute drive down to fifteen by breaking every speed limit there is. The need to see her, to touch her is borderline insane. My infatuation with her has only grown more over the last two days. Judging by Easton impatiently tapping his leg, he feels the same.

While stuck in the house, I checked to see if she had any type of social media, and of course, she didn't. And all over again, I'm reminded of how different she is in comparison to the other girls at Blackthorn.

My thoughts fade to the back of my mind, and as soon as we pull into her neighborhood, I feel like something is off. I can't put my finger on it yet, but there is something wrong. Turning on to her street, I spot it right away.

"Fucking Christ," Easton mumbles and shakes his head, his leg bouncing faster and faster, giving his uneasiness over the situation away.

Slowly, I pull up closer to Stella's house... or where it used to be. All that's left now is a pile of black ash and rubble.

What the hell happened?

I park right in front of the pile of burned wood, my mind moving a million miles a minute, questions swirl, and burn at the tip of my tongue. We just sit in the car, neither one of us saying a word as we stare at what used to be a house. The air is thick, making it hard to breathe, and my stomach rolls. I'm aware I shouldn't really feel anything for this girl, not when our plan was to torment her and keep her quiet, but that's the least of our worries now.

My gaze catches on something, and that thing has my stomach-churning. *Flowers.* Among the destruction are a set of bright flowers. They stick out like a sore thumb. I notice then that someone brought a wreath and set it next to the mailbox. I'm not stupid. People only bring flowers and wreaths for one thing: remembrance, which means...

I can't even think about it. Someone died. No, not someone. *Stella.* Fuck, I can't comprehend the thought. Dead? There is a tightening in my chest, the emotions pushing to the surface. All I can do is think as I sit there staring at what should be her house.

I should be glad that she's dead, one less person to worry about telling our secret. I should be cracking open a cold one, celebrating this easy out the universe has dropped into my lap. In reality, it feels like I've lost something... precious. I can't fully explain it, just that there is this missing piece where something used to be.

"Call your dad," Easton breaks the silence, his face void of emotion. "He has to know something."

Of course, why didn't I think of that? Probably because I was too shocked to think of anything else. Pulling out my phone, I dial my father's number. A moment later, his gruff voice comes through the speaker.

"Hello, son, staying out of trouble today?" My father asks humorously.

"Hey, Dad. Yeah, I am, but I need something... Can you tell me what happened to the house on 2nd Street?"

"Are you talking about the house that burned down?" My father asks, casually.

"Yeah, that one. Did someone die?" The words feel like shards of glass on my tongue.

"Why? Surely you don't know anyone in that neighborhood."

"I do actually... a girl I sometimes see," I admit.

"Oh, well. I don't know the whole story; I had the PR guys deal with it. I only know one body was found but couldn't be identified, and one older lady was brought to the hospital. Fire marshal says the lady set her own house on fire. Dementia or some shit. That's all I know." Inky dread pumps through my veins. Grams started the house on fire and Stella... my jaw aches with the pressure from clenching it so hard. She died because of it.

"Oh, okay. Well, thanks, Dad."

"Anytime." He hangs up the phone, and I drop my own into my lap, twisting to face Easton, who looks a little ashen.

"I mean... we should be glad she's dead. It's one less person we have to deal with. She definitely won't tell anyone who killed James now." I try to make light of the ordeal, but a sourness fills my mouth at the thought of talking about her like this.

"Look, shit happens," Easton says, "can't get hung up on some girl. It's done, people die, nothing we can do about it. Let's go to Night Shift and find someone we can screw. I doubt we'll even remember this chick come tomorrow." Easton tries to cover up his emotions with our usual activity, but I can see he is struggling. He might not show it, but he is.

"You sure that's what you want to do?" I ask, giving him a chance to right his wrong. I'm not fond of the thought of fucking Stella's memory from my brain, but what the fuck else is there to do about it?

"Yeah, I'm sure. Don't be a pussy. Let's go fuck our way through some girls and forget that she ever existed. She wasn't anyone important anyway."

I nod and swallow around the knot that's forming in my throat. I want to tell him he's being a stupid prick, but there isn't any point in arguing with him. He's hurt, and this is his way of hiding it, of dealing with the pain.

Starting the car up, I drive in the direction of Night Shift, wondering if I'll ever truly be able to forget about Stella.

～

ARRIVING AT NIGHT SHIFT, we walk in as we always do, straight to the bar for a beer. We barely sit down before the girls flock to us, knowing that we always leave a wad of cash behind for them. They're all pretty in an extremely fake way with their fake lashes, tits, and painted on faces, and normally I wouldn't be bothered by that, but tonight I need something else.

Easton reads my mind because he opens his mouth to speak before I can, "You ladies are nice and all, but we're looking for something a little different tonight."

Bridget, a girl I know by name because I request her every time I come in, starts to pout. She sucks cock like a vacuum cleaner, but that's not what I want today. I mean, I want my cock sucked but not by her.

"Oh, come on, Cam." Bridget runs her red painted nails across my chest.

"He'll be coming, but not by you," Easton chuckles.

"Are you sure? Remember that thing I do with my tongue?" She leans in and presses her body into mine, making it hard for me to ignore her presence. I can practically see her nipples through the skimpy getup she has on, and I'm tempted to lean down and suck one into my mouth. Then something off in the distance catches my eye. Blonde hair, the color of sunshine, acts as a beacon drawing my attention away from Bridget.

My heart starts to thud inside my chest like it's trying to escape it. *It can't be? Can it?* Sweat beads my brow, and I shove Bridget back and take a step forward as if that's going to help me get a better look. The girl I'm staring at has her back to me, and I wait with bated breath for her to turn around.

The muscles in my stomach tighten, and like a silent prayer, God answers me, and the nameless girl turns around, her soft gray eyes scan the room nervously, and I swear the air in my lungs stills. *Holy fucking shit.*

"Easton," I somehow get his name out. He looks over at me and away from the brunette that's seconds away from crawling into his lap.

"What? I'm trying to get my dick wet," he growls in frustration, and all I do is lift my hand, pointing in Stella's direction. He turns, and within seconds, his face softens. Then he looks, well... he looks like how I feel.

Like I've just seen a fucking ghost.

"She's alive?" He speaks so low I almost don't hear him.

"Yes, it's... it's her." I can tell, not just because of her hair or her eyes, but the perfectly sculpted shape of her body, plus she's wearing more clothing than even the bartender. She screams innocence in a place like this. Half of the guys in here are staring at her, inviting her to come closer with their eyes.

Any other girl in her would already be on someone's lap, but Stella just stands there, looking thoroughly out of place. Like a damn lamb being led to the slaughterhouse.

The uneasiness that rested heavily on my shoulders disappears in an instant. She's alive, she's fucking alive, and she's... fuck, she's working at Night Shift.

Easton's gaze turns to me. "We have to get her. She's ours." He speaks the words as if he didn't just say we should try and forget her.

"I thought you were trying to forget her," I tease, wanting to see him lose it a little. Knowing that he cares for Stella as I do, only intensifies my feelings for her more.

"Shut the fuck up," he elbows me hard in the side, "it's time to make it known that she belongs to us. I'm tired of other people looking and touching her. It's time for us to bring her home."

"Bring her home?" I lift a questioning brow.

Easton gives me a dark smile, "Yes, it's time."

"Is that the same guy talking from an hour ago? Didn't you say she was nothing to us? I remember something along the line of we won't even remember her tomorrow?"

"Shut up, and don't look at me like that. I fucking know you think the same."

Indeed, I fucking do.

"All right then, let's make her ours."

11

STELLA

My skin is crawling, and my stomach is churning. I can feel everyone's eyes on me, their stares feel like hot irons burning my skin. I've never in my life felt so exposed, so dirty. I feel like I'm on a platter, displayed all pretty while being prepared to be eaten.

This was a mistake. I knew it the moment I walked in, but I didn't know what else to do. Nothing is going to pay as good as this place does, and Grams... she needs me. Still, I have to get out of here. I'll find another way to get the money. Keeping my eyes trained on the floor, I try to ignore the hungry looks the men in the room are giving me. I hate being looked at like I'm a steak dangling in the air in front of them. Spinning around, I start to head back to the door, I just came out of, when Katie appears out of nowhere and cuts me off.

"You look like you're about to run back to the dressing room."

How did she know?

Not wanting to break down into a full mental breakdown, I force the words to come out slowly. "Because I am. I can't do this, Katie. I can't take everybody looking at me, watching me, and staring at me like I'm an alien with three eyes."

"You'll get used to it, I promise, and maybe someday you'll like it. Being the center of attention and having all the men drool over you. It's kind of a high that you can't get anywhere else, well besides drugs."

Yeah, I don't care. I'll never like having the spotlight on me. Thinking I could handle this... I'm stupid, so stupid.

"I'm sorry. It's just not for me."

"Don't be sorry," she shrugs. "I get it, you're shy. If you want to head out, I'll tell Martie you left."

"Thank you, that would be great." I almost sigh, happy that she didn't try and push me to go back out there.

"No problem. Hope you find a different job." *God, me too.*

I give her a weak smile before brushing past her and into the dressing rooms. My fingers are already at the door handle when someone taps me on the shoulder, making me jump about three feet off the ground.

"Where do you think you're going?" A deep gruff voice meets my ears. I spin around to find Martie, the club's manager towering over me.

"Ah... I-I'm sorry. I need to go. This is not for me—"

"You can go after you give this guy a lap dance. Room two," Martie orders, pointing to the small rooms in the back. With my mouth gaping open, I look back there. Did he just say lap dance? I've danced before, but never in a sexual way. I know this is what I came here for, but now that I'm here and actually supposed to do it, I just don't think I have it in me.

"I... I can't."

"You can, and you will! This is one of our best customers, and he is paying double. So, get in there and shake your ass for him. I'll let you keep $200 plus whatever tip they leave, and then you can go home."

I want to object again but know simply from the stern look Martie is giving me that it isn't worth the effort.

"Okay," I answer, my bottom lip wobbling. Bile rises in my throat, as I turn and walk toward the doors he just pointed to. It's only a lap dance, not like I'm dancing for an entire audience, and the other girls say I can always leave my panties on. So, all I have to show are my boobs. They're just boobs, not a big deal, right? I can do this. I mean, what choice do I have?

By the time I reach the door, I've not calmed down any, and in fact, I am shaking now. I swallow down the anxiousness that's threatening to suffocate me and twist the doorknob, pushing the door open. The room is dark except for a dim light that shines like a spotlight in the center of the room.

I don't know what it is about the darkness, but something about it has the panic inside me mounting. I can't do this. I take a step back and twist around at the same time, trying to get away. My escape plan is cut short when Martie appears out of nowhere, cutting off my path of escape.

"I said to get in there," he yells.

With his arms folded over his chest, he makes himself look even bigger and stronger than he probably is, and I know I don't have a chance of fighting him. He will squish me like a fly. My only option is to do as he says.

Defeated, I whisper, "Okay." The words haven't even fully left my lips when he shoves me into the dark room. I hear someone growl from inside, but I'm too busy trying to keep my balance to see where it came from, or from *who* it came from. I can barely walk in these high heels as it is, and the sudden movement has me tripping over my own feet. Instead of stepping into the small room, I tumble in, landing flat on my ass. Pain radiates up my spine, and I groan in pain.

Shit, that hurt.

"Get up," a familiar voice orders. I turn to where the voice is coming from. My eyes are adjusting to the dark now as I make out two large bodies sitting on a dark couch across the room. "I said, get up," the voice insists again, and only then does it click. The deep, cruel, darkness that accompanies that voice. It slithers through me like a snake leaving behind a slimy feeling.

Cameron and Easton.

My true living nightmares. I don't know if I should be relieved or more scared that it's them and not some old, bald guy. Getting to my feet, my shaky legs barely keep me upright as I readjust the short dress I'm wearing. I wonder how they found me, or if they are just frequent visitors of this place, that it was fate that brought us together.

"Take the dress off and start dancing," Easton growls, his voice like claws dragging across my skin. Not quite piercing the skin but leaving a red mark behind. Some song I don't know starts playing on cue, but I'm too terrified to move, let alone dance.

When I don't start moving, Cameron gets up from his seat and crosses the space between us in two long strides. Before I know what's happening, he's tugging on my dress, pulling it down my body, leaving me in nothing but some skimpy lingerie the girls let me borrow.

When my dress is pooling around my ankles, Cam steps around me and undoes my bra. He pushes it off my shoulders but doesn't let it fall to the ground. Instead, he surprises me by pulling my arms back.

"What are you doing?" I gasp, twisting to see.

"Teaching you a lesson," he smirks and starts tying my wrists with the bra while I stand there like a deer caught in the headlights, letting it happen. "You still don't seem to get it. You belong to us. No one touches you, and no one sees your body. Only us. You all but asked for a war showing up in this place. Do you want us to have to kill another person?" A shudder of fear rips across my skin.

"I just—"

"Shut up," Easton barks out, the threatening tone making me flinch.

Cameron grabs the back of my neck, leading me to where Easton is sitting. When I'm right in front of him, Cam grabs my arm with his free hand and lowers me to the ground, so I'm on my knees between Easton's legs. I wince when my bare knees make contact with the cold floor, but the guys ignore my obvious discomfort.

"Now be a good girl and suck him off," Cam orders, pushing my head toward Easton's lap, while he starts to undo his pants. "And remember what I said, he is not going to give you control like I did. Prepare yourself now."

Easton shakes his head, and a cold shiver runs down my spine. Fear wraps around my throat, making it hard to swallow. I watch nervously as Easton frees his very large and very erect cock. *It's not going to happen.* No way is he going to fit in my mouth. I've only ever done this once, and Cameron barely fit.

Distracted by Easton's cock, I don't notice until it's too late that Cam is moving to kneel behind me, he dips his fingers into my panties and pulls them down my thighs.

"Wait!" I yelp, panic clogging my throat. This cannot be how I'm going to lose my virginity. I'm not ready. "Please, not here. I'm not ready yet." I refuse to let this happen in a strip club, I already feel dirty and cheap by being here. This cannot be where I lose this part of me.

Cam's hot breath fans against my skin, his hard body presses against mine as he whispers into the shell of my ear, "You don't make the rules, sweetheart."

"We don't care if you are ready," Easton adds, his voice holding no mercy, "but if it makes you feel better, Cam won't take your virginity right now. That pleasure is reserved for me. I'm gonna be the one to pop your cherry... and I'm going to do so very soon. But right now, I just want to fuck your throat."

Before I can object, Easton grabs my head and pulls me toward him. With my hands bound behind my back, I lose my balance, and my body falls forward, but thankfully, Cam grabs my hips and steadies me.

"Open up," Easton growls, and I instantly follow his command. The soft tip of his mushroom head touches my tongue, making him groan out in pleasure. The sound vibrates through my entire body, from the tip of my tongue all the way down to my toes. I don't understand the feelings that I get when they touch me. It feels wrong, but right. Easton cradles my head with both of his hands and pulls me down, filling my mouth completely.

At the same time, one of Cameron's hands trails from my hip and down to my ass, sending little jolts of pleasure through my body. I'm completely at their mercy. If Cam wanted to, he could take me right here, right now. A thrill rushes through me at the thought. I'm scared, but just on the brink of panic, because deep down, I know they won't really hurt me.

With their hands on my body and Easton's cock in my mouth, I feel like my senses are in overdrive, and my brain is about to explode. Pushing every thought, every worry, and every fear out of my head, I try to just feel, to let them bring me pleasure, and let myself make them feel the same. Closing my eyes, I concentrate on the here and now.

Easton steadily moves deeper and deeper into my mouth with each thrust. Holding my head in place, he starts to piston his hips as much as he can in this sitting position. His cock hits the back of my throat with each thrust, and I begin to gag around his massive length. Cam was right, Easton isn't about giving control, he likes to maintain all of it.

I almost start to panic, but just when I think I'm about to lose it, Cameron runs his hand from my ass down between my legs, distracting me, forcing me to feel his fingers and swallow Easton's cock. His fingers run through my already wet folds, and when he makes contact with my swollen clit, I moan around Easton's cock.

Before his touch, I didn't even realize how much I was turned on by this. Them controlling me, using my body, making me into their slave, it awakens a dark thrill inside of me. There is something so alluring about that, letting go, losing control, and allowing someone else to make all the decisions for me. It feels... freeing. Like a weight has been lifted off my shoulders.

All the stiffness in my limbs and the shaking in my legs disappears when I let go and allow myself to feel and live in the moment, I realize that this is what I need, I relax into both of their touches. I give myself over to them, fully and completely. Body and mind. Letting them guide me in every way they see fit.

"That's it, relax your throat," Easton encourages right before upping his pace. My core tightens, and warmth moves outward through my body as he truly fucks my throat now. His deep thrusts cause saliva to build in my mouth and drip out of the corners of my lips. Tears escape the corners of my eyes, and trail down my cheeks, while my lungs burn as I force myself to breathe through my nose.

The small room is filled with a mixture of my gagging and Easton's groaning. My entire body is melting into a puddle of mind-blowing pleasure, and then Cameron's fingers enter me from behind, and my channel squeezes around his thick digit, my thighs quivering in response. Who knew it could feel this good?

"I'm gonna come down your throat, and you better take it. I want you to swallow every drop I give you," Easton orders, his cock swelling, seeming to grow even thicker in my mouth.

Cam adds a second finger then, stretching me and making me moan around Easton's length. His other hand snakes around my body and cups one of my breasts. As soon as he starts playing with the hard bud between his fingers, I feel myself start to come undone. The tingle deep in my core expanding. A match seconds away from being struck.

My head swims with the lack of oxygen as Easton shoves his cock so far down my throat I can't breathe, and still, I don't panic. In this moment, I trust them, him. Right now, I don't care about anything besides the feelings they're evoking from within me.

"Fuck..." Easton growls, halting for a moment, while deep in my throat. I can feel a warmth at the back of my throat as he comes, and this sets off my own orgasm.

Like a wildfire ready to burn down the entire forest, pure bliss blazes through me. My back arches, and my head falls back. Easton releases me, and his cock drags out over my tongue, leaving his salty release behind. The taste is so erotic, I can't help but want more.

Closing my lips around him, I suck the tip of his dick right before he pulls it out of my mouth, a small popping sound filling the room. Cameron keeps his fingers inside of me, gently stroking me until the last tremors of my release have left my body.

"Fucking Christ," Easton groans, his head tipped back. "I didn't think it would be that good, but you know how to suck a cock, Stella."

Cameron helps me straighten back up before untying my wrists. As I come down from the high, and my head and thoughts slowly clear, all the feelings I had pushed down come crashing back into me with a vengeance.

All the hurt, guilt, and fear come rushing back, threatening to swallow me whole. I can't escape the feelings any longer. It feels like this is all my fault. Me being here, the house burning down, Grams in the hospital, that woman dying in the fire. It's all my fault, I'm responsible for Grams, and I wasn't there. Someone died because of me.

Even though I'm already on my knees, I can't hold my body up. I'm too weak, too far gone mentally.

Lowering myself all the way to the ground, I curl into the fetal position and start crying like a baby. Sob after sob wrecks my body, dragging me down deeper and deeper into hopelessness.

12

EASTON

My mouth pops open as I stare at Stella, huddled like a wounded animal on the floor. *What the hell?* Nothing ruins a perfectly good blowjob like crying. And this wasn't just a good blowjob, this was heaven. I've never felt anything like this. It was pure bliss, perfection in every way, and now... she is fucking crying.

"Stella?" Cam whispers, reaching for her like she might disappear into the floor. She flinches away from him, and for the first time in my life, I'm unsure of what to do. Most would say I don't have a heart, and they would be half right because I do have a heart, I just learned how to turn off the feeling coming with it. I'm a master at disconnecting what I feel but seeing Stella crying on the floor at my feet tugs at something inside of me.

Leaning forward, I tuck my cock back into my pants and move to the edge of the couch. Staring down at Stella, all I can make out are her soft sobs. She sounds completely defeated, and all I want to do in that moment is make her feel okay. I'm a twisted son of a bitch, but I have a weakness for this girl, one that's probably going to come and bite me in the ass at some point.

"Sit up, Stella," I order, a little harsher than necessary. She doesn't move and instead starts to sob harder. Trying a different tact, I lean down, slide my arms under her body, and lift her up. I take note of the fact that she weighs barely anything at all, and a possessive urge to shove food down her throat blooms inside of my chest.

With her chin tucked into her chest, I can't see her face, but I don't have to see it to know that she's broken. Like a bird with clipped wings, she can never escape us, or what happened to her.

Taking her by the chin, I gesture for Cam to hold her up. His arms replace mine, and I force her to look at me. Big eyes misted with tears meet my own, and it feels like someone has kicked me right in the fucking balls. Pure defeat reflects back at me, and I clench my jaw to hide the emotions I'm feeling.

"What's wrong? Why are you crying? You came, did you not? I didn't hurt you." I force myself to keep my voice even and soft like I'm speaking to a child.

"I did, and you didn't hurt me." Her bottom lip wobbles and she tries to pull out of my grasp, but I pinch her chin hard, my gaze hardening. She should know better than to try and pull away by now.

"Okay, so what's the problem?"

"Aside from the obvious fact of your house burning down," Cam adds, and I shoot him a look which he dismisses with a smirk.

"I...I... It's all my fault. I should have been home. I should have been with her."

"Your grandma is sick, that's not your fault, and you can't always be with her, so stop blaming yourself," I tell her the truth, but she keeps crying, probably not even hearing much of what I say.

"The doctor at the hospital said Grams needs to be put in a home. One of those fancy expensive ones where she has doctors and nurses around the clock." Stella blinks away some of the tears and lets out a shuddering breath. "I started working here because it's the only job I can get where I'll be able to afford something like that for her."

I nod, understanding her need to protect her grandmother. She's all she has, but I refuse to let her work here, to let her show her body off to any Joe Blow that walks in this place. No fucking way. She's ours.

"You know we won't let you work here, right?" I reply, and the sadness in her eyes returns ten-fold. She nods her head as best she can, her lips start trembling again.

"Not because we don't want you to have a chance at making money and taking care of your grams, but because you belong to us," Cam tells her, his voice dropping to a panty-melting degree, "and no way in hell are we letting someone look, let alone touch you."

Like a dam breaking, Stella falls apart, big fat tears start to roll down her cheeks again. Never before was it so apparent to me how complicated women are. I just fucked 'em and left. What the hell do I do now?

"I have nowhere to go... I'm staying in a motel right now that I can barely afford."

Her confession sets the alpha off inside of me.

"A Motel? Where?"

"Not far from here," she answers through sobs.

Before I can put too much thought into what I'm saying, the words just pour out of me, "You're not going back there. You're staying with us." This causes her gaze to widen and her swollen lips to part. I know that Stella isn't just anyone to us and that until we've had our fill of her, she will be ours to do whatever we want with.

"Stt-staying with you? I don't even know where you're staying? Plus, I can't. I have no money. I can't afford it." Panic visibly claws at her throat, and I hate seeing her like this. Breaking eye contact with Stella, I meet Cam's concerned gaze. I know what he wants to do to her, wrap his arms around her and tell her everything is going to be okay. But it's not. The cruel truth of the world is that not everything is always going to be okay. Sometimes it's going to be shit, and it might be that way for a while. That's just the way the world works.

I understand how Cam is, in many ways, he is the opposite of me, soft, charismatic, and tender when he needs to be, together we're the epitome of what a man should be. But all of those things, they're not what Stella needs. She needs our strength, passion, some tender love. But most of all, she needs us to control her.

"What if we offered to pay you the same pay you get here. All you would have to do is dance for us. Exclusively."

"Dance for you?" She looks confused.

"That's what you were doing here, right? You can still do it, but for us instead."

"I don't know... I don't think I can do it. I don't want to come with you..." Her words slice through me, igniting an anger that burns hotter than the fucking sun. Before I know what I'm doing, my hand is releasing her chin and moving around to the back of her neck. In a second, my fingers splay through her soft hair wrapping around the golden strands as I grab a fist full of it. She yelps out when I force her head back by her hair, exposing her delicate throat to me.

"I don't understand why you still think you have a say in anything. I try and be gentle with you, but it does me no good. It seems like you want to be controlled, want us to tell you what to do. Fortunately for you, I can make that happen." I lean into her face, making note of her wince. "I don't care what you want. You are coming with us, and you should be glad we are paying you at all because if we wanted to, we could just take from you, take until there isn't a single thing left."

"You're hurting me," she whimpers, but I don't let her go. In fact, I want to tighten my grip but reel myself in, afraid that if I lose control, I may actually harm her. She's so precious like glass, the slightest crack may shatter her.

"Stella doesn't like pain," Cameron explains, a frown on his lips. "She told me the other day that she doesn't want us to hurt her."

"Is that so?" I look away from Cameron and back down at her, "I didn't hear you complaining when I was slapping your pussy. If I recall, you creamed all over my fucking fingers. I've never seen a woman so wet in my life."

"Please, stop," she begs, and I feel her words in my cock, which is currently rising to attention. "I'll... I'll come with you. Just please don't hurt me anymore."

"Hurt you?" I growl, and release her hair, "You've yet to know what it feels like to be hurt, but I suppose it's time we showed you. Maybe we need to give you a little more pain, show you what it would feel like."

Stella starts to shake her head, big fat tears cascading down her cheeks, and I feel compelled to lick them off her face. I want to taste her fear, taste her pain.

Cameron pulls her to her feet, but as soon as he lets go of her, she looks like she is about to collapse. Both of us are on her in a flash, making sure she doesn't fall.

"Don't make this harder than it has to be. Let us take care of you. All you have to do in return is keep your pretty mouth shut, spread your legs a little, and shake your ass for us. Can you do that, sweetheart? Can you be a good girl?" Cam's voice turns seductive, and I almost grin at the effort he is using. We don't have to seduce her; she'll do whatever we want either way.

"Yes," she finally answers, defeat dripping from that one single word. Reaching into my back pocket, I take out five one-hundred-dollar bills and shove them into her hand. She lifts her gaze from the floor and to her hand before flicking her pretty eyes up to my face.

"There is way more where that came from," I grin. She doesn't say anything, but she does close her hand around the money. She might be stubborn, but she isn't stupid. She needs the money bad enough to not worry about her pride.

Together Cam and I help Stella become a little more presentable, covering her as best as we can. Cam puts his arms around her and tucks her to his side. I grin, seeing how she instinctively leans into him, seeking comfort. She might be scared of us, but part of her knows that we'll protect her.

As soon as we exit the room, I find Martie. I still want to put my fist into his face for pushing Stella in the room earlier, but I know he has like three bouncers in here who would pounce on me like the attack dogs they are.

"She is leaving with us, and she is not coming back. If you see her in here again give either Cam or me a call," I speak the words to Martie, but my eyes aren't on him, they're on Stella. In a room full of half-naked women, she is the only one I can see right now. If I was ever going to fall for a girl, it would be her.

"Got it," Martie mumbles under his breath and walks away.

Spotting Valorie eyeing us like we've lost our minds, I wave her over. When she is in earshot, I tell her, "Go fetch Stella's shit from the dressing room."

She frowns but does as I command. A few moments later, she returns, holding a plastic bag with what I assume is clothes. I grab it from her without a word, and the three of us walk out.

I can feel everyone staring at us, probably trying to figure out what makes Stella so different from the rest of the girls in this place. I've lost count of how many girls here have begged us to take them home. The first night Stella is here, we take her. Truthfully, I don't know what it is about her, but what I do know is she is ours, and nothing is going to take her away from us.

Nothing.

~

WHEN WE ARRIVE BACK at the house that we share with Warren, Stella is asleep in the backseat. Slowly I pull into the driveway and kill the engine. We've never brought a chick here other than for fucking. We are bringing Stella to stay. The thought seems ridiculous, but also completely right. It's different because we are not just making her share our bed, we are making her share our lives, and that makes this all seem ten times more personal.

Cam moves, lifting Stella into his arms, his gaze colliding with my own in the rearview mirror. I know he's getting attached, the tether tightening around his heart that connects to her. Does he not realize how slippery and fucked up love can get? Plus, we need to keep a clear head, there's still a chance she could tell someone about what we did, and if we have to hurt her, that will only complicate things.

As if he understands what I'm saying with only my eyes, he nods and opens the back door with one hand. He slips out of the car and onto the driveway, and I get out and run around to his side. Stella stirs in his arms; her big eyes flicker open and move over the landscape.

"Where are we?" She croaks.

"Our place, we share it with a friend, but he won't care if you're here or not."

Stella doesn't look like she believes us, but I don't really care what she believes or not. All she needs to worry about is us. Her sole attention and concern should be us. Cam lets her go and sets her down on her feet. She sways as if she's going to fall over but rights herself, holding her chin up high.

There is the Stella I know is hiding right beneath the surface. We walk up the front steps and into the house. Silence greets us as we step inside and close the door behind us. My hand circles her forearm as I tug her toward the bedroom. Part of me wishes I could be kinder, gentler with her, but I don't have it in me.

"Where are you taking me?" She sounds exhausted, and for once, I don't want to fight with her.

"You're going to take a shower, tell us what happened with Grams, and then we're all going to go to bed," I explain as we walk down the hall. When we reach my bedroom, I open the door and lead us inside. I release her and walk over to the dresser, pulling out a T-shirt and a pair of boxers. They'll both be big on her, but they'll have to do until we get her some clothes.

"Bathroom is right through there." I point to the second door on the right side of the room. When she doesn't say anything, I close the distance between us and give her the clothing. Cam went to his bedroom, most likely to shower and change too, so it's just her and me.

"Nothing is going to happen to you. We won't hurt you," I tell her.

"Maybe not tonight, but eventually you will. That's what you keep saying, at least."

"We told you that we would only hurt you if you don't do as we say."

"And how long is that supposed to go on? I can't just stay here with you forever. I have my own life," she whispers the last bit, her hands holding onto the clothes with a death grip. I digest what she's said, and the only answer I can come up with is one that will make this all the more confusing for her.

"You belong to us. That's all you need to know right now." I don't understand the infatuation, and I may never, but I'm tethered to her. Cam and I both are. I lean into her face, wanting to kiss her lips that are shaped in a sad frown. It doesn't matter if she's happy or sad, she still makes my cock rock hard. "Go shower, and when you get out, we will finish talking," I order.

She looks up at me hesitantly as if she doesn't believe I'd let her shower alone, but then she whips around and all but runs into the bathroom. The door closes behind her a second later, and then I hear the shower turning on.

Sighing against the king-size bed, I try and figure out what the hell we're doing. I lie there for a few minutes before I hear Cam walk into the bedroom.

"Did you kill her?" he asks jokingly. I stare at him openly like he's stupid.

"No, she's showering. Then she's going to tell us what happened with Grams and who died in the fire."

"Okay…" there is a long pause of silence, and I let my eyes drop down to the floor. "When does this end? Neither one of us does relationships. We can't possibly keep her."

His questions irritate me. Mainly because I don't know the solution, I don't know how this is going to end.

Swallowing down my anger, I tell myself he's just thinking rationally, "I don't have an answer, and I don't know what's going to happen. I'm just taking it all one day at a time." We share a secret and letting her go now would be like cutting off my own hand. It would hurt, and I would know there was a missing piece. I wouldn't die, and I could easily live, but why cut off a perfectly good hand?

"I get it, but this isn't fair to her. I mean, what's…" Anger boils over inside of me, and I twist on the bed to face him, cutting him off.

"Life isn't fair, Cam. Don't let your feelings for her cloud your judgment. Think with your big head, and not your little one."

Cam gives me a dirty look, his mouth popping opening before he closes it, holding in his response when the bathroom door opens, and Stella's towel-covered head pops out. She tiptoes out of the bathroom and I take in her slender body. Something catches my eye on her neck; it's then that I see the bruises on her throat. She must have covered them up with makeup before, they were definitely not visible earlier.

Pure rage pumps through my veins, and I'm half tempted to get back in my car and go find Paul to make sure he doesn't try and hurt her again.

"Come sit," I pat the spot on the bed beside me, pushing my anger for Paul aside. Stella looks between both of us before she starts moving. I let my gaze linger over her legs, and her middle, which is currently swallowed by my T-shirt.

Fuck, she looks good in my clothes. A possessive need to toss her on the bed and ravage her alive roars to the surface, but I tamp it down, knowing her day has been rough enough.

"What's going to happen next?" She mumbles softly.

"For now, just tell us what happened, and if you're hungry, we can get some food. After that, we'll go to bed."

"I don't have to sleep with you?"

"Well, you will sleep with me in my bed, but that's all we'll do today. No fucking tonight. That's coming soon though," Cam grins at her, and I swear all the blood in her face drains. I place my hand on her knee and squeeze it gently, bringing her attention back to me.

"Tonight, nothing happens. Just tell me what went down at the house. Grams is in the hospital, and you're alive, so who was the person that died?"

Stella sniffles and I wonder if she's going to start crying again. God, I'm not sure I can handle any more tears tonight. "Our neighbor went in and saved Grams, and we are guessing she thought I was inside too. That's why she went back in. They couldn't get her out in time."

"How did the fire start?" I ask.

"Grams was cooking again and forgot to turn the stove off after." Tears well in her gray eyes. "The police called me while I was job searching, they came and got me, took me to the hospital. When I got there, they told me..." Emotions clog her throat, and she takes a calming breath forcing air into her lungs. "They said Grams is a danger to herself, me, and others. She needs to be put in a home where she can be watched and cared for around the clock."

"All that matters is that she's okay. Like we said, we'll pay you enough to help take care of her. We're assholes, but not heartless," Cam chuckles, but neither Stella nor I laugh.

"I don't even have clothes. The only things I have are in that bag, it's what I was wearing the day of the fire." Avoiding my eyes, she looks down at her bare legs.

"Don't worry about that. We'll get you some clothes and whatever else you need as well. We take care of what's ours," I tell her, but she doesn't seem to find much comfort in my words.

"Come on, let's get you to bed," Cameron says, motioning for her to get up. She stands up and starts following him out of my room, but before she gets to the door, she pauses and turns to me one more time. She doesn't say anything, just looks at me. I can't for the life of me figure out what the hell she is thinking right now. Then she turns back to Cam and disappears from my room like she wasn't here at all.

13

STELLA

I wake up slowly, from a sleep that has been the deepest and the best sleep I've had in a very long time. The mattress feels like a cloud, and the sheets are so incredibly soft on my skin; they feel like silk. But the most comfortable and soothing part of this bed is the warmth like a protective cocoon it wraps around me, protecting me and keeping me safe.

My eyes flutter open, and it takes my foggy mind a moment to realize where the hell I am. The room is mostly dark, only a small sliver of light peeks through the blackout curtains covering the windows.

The mattress and sheets are still soft, but the protective cocoon I envisioned quickly turns into something else entirely when I realize what I'm cuddling into. It's Cameron's body wrapped around my own.

Dread replaces the fuzzy, comfortable feeling in my chest. How can I sleep in his arms... in his bed, so peacefully? I should recoil, not lean into him.

I try to inch away from him, but his arm around me seemingly weighs a hundred pounds, keeping me pinned to the bed, and tucked against his chest.

"Where do you think you're going?" Cam asks, his face so close to my neck that his breath tickles my skin there. A shiver runs down my spine, and he tucks me into his chest even closer. "Are you cold?"

"No," I whisper. "And I was trying to get up," I answer his first question.

"And do what?"

"Nothing. I was just..."

"Trying to get away from me?" He finishes the sentence for me.

"Can you blame me?" The words pour out before I can stop them.

"Yes, I can," he chuckles. "You should know better than to try to get away. Plus, you have no real reason to."

"Other than you threatening me every day since we met?"

"As long as you behave, nothing will happen to you. You should be glad that we found you last night. Would you rather work at the Night Shift? Sleep in that shithole you called a motel? You should be thankful that you are here, sleeping in a nice bed."

"Don't pretend you have me here out of the goodness of your heart. The only reason I'm here is because you want to use me... use my body. At least at the strip club, I could make my own decisions. Make my own choices."

"And where have those led you? You don't want to pretend? Fine, then we won't. We won't pretend that you don't enjoy what we do to you." He flips me around in his arms, so I have to look at his face before he continues, "We won't pretend that you don't moan every time we touch you, that you don't push your pussy against my hand when I slide my fingers into you. And we won't pretend you didn't enjoy the taste of Easton's come as you sucked the last drop from his cock, or that you didn't come so hard, your whole body quivered."

"Stop," I whimper, again trying to pull away from him. I don't want to hear any of this.

"Why? Because it's true?"

Shame coats my inside as I'm faced with the fact that he is right. They might not have given me a choice, but the truth of the matter is,

I did enjoy what they did to me. I enjoyed them taking control. I want to be theirs in more than one way.

What does that say about me? Is there something wrong with me for wanting something so filthy and bad?

"This is all wrong," I whine. "I didn't ask for any of this."

"We didn't either, but here we are. It doesn't matter how we got here. You are ours now, and the faster you come to terms with that, the better. So, why don't we go and see if Easton is up so we can make you officially ours." Cameron moves off the bed, pulling me along with him.

"Wait...what are we doing?"

"You know what we're *doing*." Cam grins and a knot starts to form inside my gut, and yet there is this warmth that I feel at the thought of being claimed by them. God, this is wrong and confusing. Taking me by the hand, he leads me out of his room and across the hall and into Easton's room. Cameron doesn't even knock. He just barges in like he owns the place. Entering Easton's room, we find him still lying in his bed.

I expect him to still be asleep, but he isn't. Instead, he's looking at something on his phone. He looks up and shoots both of us a questioning look before dropping the phone onto the mattress next to him.

"Well, what a nice morning surprise," he smirks like the devil as he sits up and stretches his arms above his head.

"I think Stella is ready for you. It's time to pop that cherry between her legs and make her ours for good." Cam gives me a gentle shove toward the bed. Easton smiles so widely, I think I can see every single one of his perfectly straight white teeth.

Oh no, I'm being led to the slaughterhouse.

"Don't look so scared, I'll make sure it's good for you too," Easton coos, his warm hand circles my wrist and he tugs me toward him. With no other option, I climb up on his bed, glancing back at Cameron, who is standing at the foot of the bed, watching like a hawk ready to swoop in at any given second.

"Do you want me to stay?" he asks, taking me by surprise. They usually don't ask me for my opinion, so I didn't see the question coming at all.

"I don't know," I answer, truthfully.

Do I want him to be here? I never expected to have two guys in the room with me when I lost my virginity, but of course, I didn't think there would be two guys fingering me, or two guys while I gave one a blowjob. I'm so used to having them both, that sending Cam away seems wrong.

"Stay," Easton prompts his friend, before grabbing the hem of my shirt and pulling it up and over my head. Cool air washes over my now naked chest, turning my nipples into small hard pebbles. Even though I know deep down it's wrong, I'm turned on. I want their darkness, their hands on me. I want both of them together, and I think my biggest problem is the fact that I keep denying it, hoping my feelings will change, but they don't.

Easton interrupts my train of thought when his mouth latches onto one of my hardened nipples. He sucks hard, his eyes locked on mine as pleasure starts to pulse between my legs at the first flick of his tongue. In a second, I can feel everything. His hands splayed across my back, goosebumps pebble my flesh as he pulls me closer, and I tip my head back, a soft whimper escaping my lips.

"That's the thing about you, Stella," Easton croaks his voice filled with lust after he releases my nipple and eyes the other breast. "Even when you aren't sure if it's right in your head, your body makes it right. Deep down, you know you belong to us; you just don't want to admit it."

My toes curl into the mattress when he sucks my other nipple into his mouth and teases me with hard bites and sensual sucks.

By the time he's done with both breasts, I'm panting with need, every cell in my body on fire. Moving me back against the mattress, he dips his fingers into the shorts he gave me last night and pulls them down my legs.

He moves so slowly it's almost as if he's enjoying every second of this. He looks at me like I'm something precious. Like he actually cares about how this feels for me. But that can't be right. Easton doesn't care about me.

My gaze moves from Easton and back to Cameron, who has found a chair in the corner of the room. Our eyes lock, and the fire in my center roars, growing hotter. Easton pinches one of my nipples hard, dragging my attention back to him.

"Eyes on me, sweetheart. I'm about to rock your fucking world." He grins and tosses my clothing onto the floor. His eyes turn to molten lava as he rakes over my bare flesh. There isn't a single inch of me that I can hide from him. I feel exposed, but at the same time cherished, protected. I know that neither of them will let anything happen to me.

"Innocent, perfect. I can't wait to dirty you up. To show you how good this can be." I shiver at the darkness that coats his words and watch with an eagerness that is embarrassing as he strips for me, first removing his shirt and then next his sleep pants. My eyes automatically drift down to his already hard and throbbing cock.

And just like that, panic starts to claw its way back into my mind. How is he going to fit? Is it going to hurt? Is he going to take me like a savage? I'm consumed with these thoughts so much so that I flinch when Easton's fingers graze my lips.

"Stop thinking, and just feel," he whispers as he leans into my face, his hot breath fanning against my lips.

"I'm scared," I admit, almost shyly. I don't know why I say it, it's not like it matters. He'll just take from me, even if it hurts me.

"Do you trust me?" His eyes burn into mine.

I should say no, but stupidly I nod my head yes because something inside of me is convinced that I can. I do trust him, even if I shouldn't. With a sinister smile, he trails his finger down my body, blazing a path of fire, one that only his touch can extinguish.

Pushing my knees apart, he moves his fingers over my mound, swiping through my folds. His eyes ignite with a furious need when my arousal coats his fingers. All I can do is whimper as he moves lower and presses two thick digits against my entrance.

My stomach clenches as he enters me, stretching me so very slowly. Warmth fills my veins as he moves in and out, the sound of my arousal only turns me on more, and I find myself wrapping my hand around his wrist, encouraging him to go faster.

His chest rises and falls rapidly, while his eyes darken in color. Caught in a trance of pleasure, I let him fuck me with his fingers, moving faster and faster until I'm right on the doorstep of an orgasm.

"Come for me, baby. Squeeze my fucking fingers, show me how good you're going to be to my cock," Easton encourages, as he rubs at this unknown spot inside of me that has my eyes drifting closed and my back bowing. I don't understand the pleasure coursing through me in that instant, but it's so intense that the world could stop spinning right now, and I wouldn't care.

"Ohhhh," I whine. "It's sooo good." Like a rocket, my orgasm takes off, and I clamp down on his fingers, squeezing them so tightly I evoke a groan out of Easton. My mind swirls into one big mass, not one single thought making any sense.

As I float back down to reality, he pulls his fingers from my entrance, and my eyes pop open just as he's shoving them into his mouth, licking every drop of my release from them.

"You taste divine," he says around his fingers.

My cheeks heat at the image, and my entire body ignites. I spot Cam over in the corner, his eyes half-lidded, his cock out with his hand wrapped around it tightly. He gives me a soft smile, and my heart starts to beat a little harder.

Wrong. This is wrong. But it feels right, so right.

Easton moves between my legs, spreading me wider. An entire

kaleidoscope of butterflies takes flight in my stomach as he pumps his thick cock in his hand, pre-come glistening against the tip.

As he leans forward, guiding his length toward my entrance, I clamp up.

"Wait, I'm..."

Easton pauses with his jaw clenched. He doesn't look mad, just unhinged like he wants to slam into me instead of stopping. His muscles tremble as he stares down at me.

"I'm not on birth control," I croak out.

The words must penetrate somewhere in his mind because he nods then, "I'll pull out, but by the end of the week, you'll be on birth control." He's not asking, he's telling me.

Nodding, I watch as he exhales, and grapples for control over himself. My nipples harden, and my stomach tightens with anticipation. He presses a feather-light kiss to my top lip, as he moves closer, the head of his cock moves through my folds, gathering up my arousal. Then he's there, at my entrance. Gently he presses against me, and I can feel the resistance my body puts up at his sheer size, but like the beast he is, Easton gives no fucks and thrusts inside of me with one swivel of his hips.

The air in my lungs stills, and my nails sink into his shoulders as pain ripples through my midsection. Easton tips his head back and lets out a low growl as I clench down around him.

"Holy fuck, I knew it would be good."

For a whole second, he doesn't move, and I'm thankful because I'm barely keeping it together. The pain starts to recede, and Easton starts to thrust slowly inside of me, his eyes pierce mine as he does, intensifying the moment.

His pelvis grinds against my clit with each move of his hips, and the combination is mind-blowing. All I can feel is him, under my skin, in my soul. It's like he's consuming me, and I want him to. I want him to take and take until there is nothing left.

"You feel so good." He shudders against me. "You feel it too, don't you?"

All I can do is nod my head as he starts to move faster and faster, each thrust sending a jolt of pleasure through me. Pressing his head into the crook of my neck, he sucks on the tender flesh just above my pulse.

"Easton," I mewl, clawing at his back like a wild animal. My nails scrape against his skin, sinking deeply, so deep I wonder if I've drawn blood.

"Come apart for me. I want to feel you milk my cock. I want to feel your release coat my balls. Come for me, Stella…" He grunts into my throat. And even if I didn't want to, there is no way I couldn't. I'm too far gone to care about anything else in that instant.

Like a bird taking flight, I jump over the cliff's edge as Easton swivels his hips, pressing just enough friction to my clit. My entire body shakes as it's overcome with pleasure that consumes every fiber of my body. Warmth seeps in my bones, and I'm only vaguely aware of Easton grunting and growling like an animal as he moves faster and faster, his muscles rippling as he ruts into me.

"So good, so fucking good," he snarls.

I'm slowly coming down from my orgasm when he starts to come. His cock seems to grow bigger inside of me, and I open my mouth to tell him to pull out, but it's too late. I can already feel his sticky warm come coating the inside of my womb. His cock pulses as he continues to fill me with every last drop of his release, and while I feel sedated, I can't help but feel that little bit of worry at the back of my mind.

Completely spent, Easton sags against me, and strangely, I love the feel of his body weight against me. In his arms, I feel safe and secure.

"You did good, baby," Easton coo's into my ear and presses a gentle kiss to my forehead as he pulls away from me. His cock slips out of my pussy, and I wince, a dull ache replacing the amazement that was just there.

My eyes hone in on the blood that's covering his cock. I lost my virginity. I gave my virginity to a man I'm pretty sure I'm falling for. A man that is a killer, a heartless bastard.

"It's just a little blood, nothing to worry about."

I'm not sure what to say about that, but as Easton moves off the bed, I become hyperaware of the fact that Cam watched us have sex. Again, I feel like I should be bothered by this, but the feeling of shame remains absent.

Cameron's hooded gaze locks on mine, and my heart does a flip in my chest at the carnal need pulsing outward from him.

"It's my turn, baby... my turn to claim your last virgin hole." He smiles, and as if I know what's to come, my pussy clenches. They weren't lying about dirtying me up.

14

CAMERON

Fuck. She's looking at me like a siren with her just fucked hair, pebbled nipples, and amazing body on display. She bites at her lower lip, and I can't actually believe what I'm seeing. She wants this. She wants me buried in her ass.

"You keep giving him fuck me eyes, and he won't take that sweet ass of yours as gently as I took your pussy." Stella doesn't even bat an eyelash at Easton's comment, and that only makes my need for her intensify. Fuck, she's doing crazy stupid things to my head. Standing, I shuck my clothes and walk to the edge of the bed.

My eyes move over the rumpled sheets and the spot just beneath her, where there is a splotch of blood. It calls to me like a beacon, and I feel like a savage as I stare down at a prize that was given to me.

"Do you want me in your ass?" I ask her, just needing to confirm.

With rosy cheeks she says, "Yes."

My heart beats into my throat as I walk over to the nightstand and pull out the bottle of lube that Easton keeps inside. Stella watches my every move like I am the hunter, and she is my prey. In many ways, that's exactly what we are. I'm the predator, and she is a helpless small animal, utterly at my mercy.

Easton takes the chair I was sitting in just moments ago while I grab a pillow and place it next to Stella.

"Turn around, pillow under your hips," I order, and watch Stella turn around eagerly. Does she not know what I have in store for her?

With the pillow under her, her ass is propped up nicely, giving me a prime view of her swollen and wet pussy, Easton's come dripping out of it. Soon she'll have come dripping out of both holes.

Popping the cap on the lube, I drip some over her ass cheeks and watch it run down her skin. Using the palm of my hand, I start rubbing it into her heated flesh, kneading her ass before I run my finger between those creamy cheeks, finding her puckered hole. She gasps when I touch it but doesn't make a move or tell me to stop.

She wants this... wants it badly.

"Just stay relaxed like you are right now," I encourage her as I start massaging her opening. It only takes me a minute of teasing before I'm able to slip my finger in with ease. "That's right, let me inside. Give me that tight ass."

I add a second finger and start pumping deeper, her tight ring of muscles squeezes me, attempting to push me out. Stella's hands fist against the sheets as she slowly pushes back against my hand. My insides twist with anxious need as I watch my fingers move in and out of her. In. Out. In. Out.

"Your ass is swallowing my fingers... is it hungry for my cock?" I ask, pressing a kiss against her ass cheek.

"Yes, please," she whimpers, clearly feeling the same burning need in her veins that I am. I pull both fingers out, and Stella whines at the loss of my touch.

"One second, baby, and you'll be so full of my cock, you won't know where I start, and you end." Popping the bottle of lube open, I pour a generous amount into my palm before coating my cock with it. I want to make this nice and easy for her, so she wants to do this again and again. Closing it, I let the bottle fall to the mattress, and I reach for her again, pressing against her lower back. Pumping my cock in my hand, I spread the lube across my entire length before bringing the head to her puckered hole.

"We own you, forever, and always," I growl as I lean over her body. The head of my cock presses against the tight hole, and I push in slowly, the ring of muscles in her ass fighting with resistance against my size. I grit my teeth and tell myself to go slow, my muscles burn, and my body is burning up with need. I have to have her. I have to claim her tight little ass. Pulling back, I thrust my hips forward, sliding all the way inside of her.

The tightness of her ass squeezing my cock causes stars to appear in my vision. I feel lightheaded. *Fuck.* Stella doesn't move or make a single peep, and I remain unmoving inside of her, letting her adjust.

"How does it feel?" I ask, slowly moving my hips.

"Full. I feel so full," she mewls.

"Do you want me to fuck you?" A long second passes, and I'm not sure what I'll do if she says no. My cock's already six inches inside of her. I could take from her, but I know this moment would never happen again, and with as good as she feels, I want to be inside her ass as often as she lets me be.

"Yes, slowly…" She purrs, looking at me over her shoulder. There's so much trust in her gray eyes part of me wants to tell her that trusting me is wrong, but I can't because deep down, I know I'll never truly hurt her. Placing both hands on her hips, I ground myself and start to move in and out of her slowly. My muscles ache with the effort it takes me not to pull out of her and pound into her tight little ass.

After a short while, she pushes back against me, encouraging me to go faster and thank fuck because my control was slipping.

Upping my pace, I swivel my hips, listening as Stella's breaths become hard pants. I'm so turned on, so ready to rut, I can feel the pressure mounting in my balls.

"Fuck, you feel too good. I'm going to end up coming soon…" I release her hips and move in and out at a vicious pace. Snaking a hand beneath our bodies, I find her swollen clit and press my thumb against it.

"Oh, oh, god. Cameron..." She gasps into the bed, and the sound is music to my ears. I continue to fuck her ass and rub against her clit, knowing she's close to going off. I can feel her entire body tightening, growing tighter and tighter as we continue toward the edge of complete bliss.

"Shit, baby, come for me, squeeze my cock with your perfect ass." I can't hold off much longer, and thank fuck she starts to come undone then.

Like a present slowly being unwrapped, she sags against the mattress and falls apart, her body trembling her release barreling into her, owning her tight little body. Her ass squeezes my cock, and I continue to pound into her until my balls tighten, and sweat beads my brow. Pleasure zings through me like lightning, and my entire body vibrates. I can't breathe. I can't see. I'm blinded by and consumed with need.

Unable to hold off my release a second longer, I let myself explode in her ass, filling her puckered hole with every drop of my sticky come.

Drifting back down from my high, I pull out of her ass, watching as come dribbles out of her ass. There is nothing as hot as seeing a woman dripping come out of both of her holes. She's been owned, and I'll be damned if we let her go ever again.

"Fuck," Easton groans from the chair, and I turn to see him jerking off, spurts of hot come erupting from his cock.

I give him my back and turn my attention to Stella, who is lying against the mattress, a melty mess of orgasms and come.

"Your ass is going to be mine again and again. It'll stretch for my cock, and eventually, you'll take both of us at the same time. You want that, don't you? Both of us fucking you at the same time? Claiming both tight holes." I tug her back by the hair and press a kiss against her forehead. She doesn't so much as say a word and only grunts in approval.

Good girl. I'm happy she's learning the rules. Learning who it is that owns her, that seals her fate.

"Roll over," I order and move away from her. She does as I say, a sleepy look appearing in her eyes. I walk into Easton's bathroom and get a washcloth, wetting it with warm water before returning to her. When I reach the bed, I find Easton beside her, his hand between her legs. He sinks two fingers inside her pussy, and I watch to see where he's going to take this next.

"We're going to leave and go to our class," he tells her, his eyes burning into hers. "You're going to stay right here. On this bed, just like this until we return."

Stella's gaze darts between us. I can see the apprehension forming there. Easton pumps in and out of her a little faster, causing her to lift her hips, seeking out pleasure.

"Shit, you're our dirty little slut, aren't you?" I hiss, my cock growing rock hard all over again. Stella nods, her teeth sinking into her pink bottom lip.

Easton slows, and she whines in disapproval, "What are you going to do?"

Stella is slow to respond, and Easton pulls all the way out, landing a hard slap against her pussy. "Oh... god... I'm going... I'm going to stay in bed. Just like this." She pants, her mouth watering and her pussy quivering with need.

Easton smiles with approval, "That's right, and you aren't going to touch this pussy. Got it? It belongs to us. Only we fuck it, eat it, and touch it, do you understand?"

"I..." Her small body trembles and her nipples are hard enough to cut glass. Easton gives her no warning as he slaps her pussy again. "Fuck..." She cries out, pleasure and pain forming in her features.

"I'm starting to think you like getting your pussy slapped. Do you understand?" Easton asks one last time.

"Yes, yes..." Stella answers completely out of breath. Her chest rises and falls rapidly, drawing my attention back to her tits. I want to fuck them, suck them. I can see the juices of her arousal dripping down her thighs. Is he going to leave her like this?

"Good." He moves away from the bed, and I can practically see the fire forming in her eyes. It flickers, fanning the flames of anger. He is. He's leaving her panting, writhing with need. "And if you touch yourself or get yourself off, we will know, and it won't end well for you. I'll draw out your next orgasm until you're begging, crying, pleading with me to make you come." The warning is clear. Touch yourself, and you'll regret it.

Easton gets dressed, and I toss the washcloth onto the mattress beside her, afraid that if I go to her, I'll be tempted to ease her pain.

"Be a good girl and stay on the bed. Sleep, because when we get back in a couple of hours, you'll need your strength," I tell her, turn around and walk out of the room. The image of her completely naked, bare, and dripping with come will stay etched into the darkest parts of my mind for a very long time.

∾

CLASSES DRAG ON, and all I want to do is get back to our place and fuck Stella all over again. Even as innocent as she is, I know there is a darkness lingering somewhere inside. A piece that begs to be fucked and consumed by Easton and me.

I want to draw that darkness out, but just a little, we have to take special care with her, so we don't dull out her light in the process.

When the professor finally dismisses us, Easton and I are the first ones out of the class. Without saying anything, I know he is thinking what I am thinking. Get home as soon as possible. Knowing that she is waiting for us, still naked, sprawled out on Easton's bed is giving me a permanent hard-on. I need to get home, and I need to do that fast.

As soon as we get to the car, I notice something is on the windshield, but I need to actually walk around to be able to see what it is. Stepping to the front of the car, I curse under my breath when I see the bright red lettering on the glass. Immediately, I look around, scanning for someone who could have done it.

"Fuck," Easton murmurs when he sees it too. "I don't think anyone has seen this. Let's go before someone does."

We both hurry, I get into the driver's seat and turn the car on. Right away, I use the windshield wipers to wipe away the writing. *I know what you did to James.*

"Who the fuck knows about that? The only other person besides us is..." Easton trails off.

"She wouldn't have. She's too scared of us."

"Is she?" Easton's question has me wondering. *Shit*, I don't want to think about it. If Stella betrayed us like that... I don't know what I would do. I don't know if I could hurt her now, not after what happened this morning.

"Let's not jump to conclusions. We'll go home and ask her. Then we'll figure it out," I say, gripping the steering wheel a little tighter.

The normal five-minute drive feels like five hours, and when I finally pull into the driveway, I sigh in relief. I kill the engine, and we both jump out of the car. Walking into the house, a dread settles deep into my bones. What if she told someone? What choice do we have besides hurting her?

With Easton right on my heels, we head to his room. I push the door open and come to a sudden halt. My eyes scan the room frantically, willing her to appear. *No!*

"You've got to be fucking kidding me," Easton growls beside me.

She's gone. She fucking left. She betrayed us.

15

STELLA

I climb off the bus and hurry down the sidewalk toward the hospital they've temporarily put Grams in. I don't know exactly what's wrong, but the nurse who called me sounded distraught. All she said was that Grams was crying and asking for me. I had never gotten dressed so quickly in my life. Leaving Cameron and Easton's house without telling them might come back to bite me in the ass later, but I can't think about that right now. I just need to see my grams, to make sure she is okay.

Walking through the spinning doors, I sprint to the front desk and ask to be taken to my grandma. She is in the closed wing of the hospital, a part that you need a code to get in. The lady at the front desk calls someone to pick me up, and I wait impatiently for that person to come.

When a heavy-set bald guy in white scrubs finally comes to get me, I all but run toward him. "Is my grams okay?"

"Yeah, I think the nurse overreacted a bit. She is new and still getting used to patients with dementia. Your grandma is doing much better now that we gave her something to calm her down." *Gave her something?* I don't really like the way that sounds, but I don't say anything.

Instead, I follow him, a bad feeling lingering in my gut as he leads me through the hospital wing. With every step I take, the bad feeling inside of me spreads, and when we finally get to Grams' room, the dread I experienced reaches a boiling point.

She is in bed, lying flat on her back, looking up at the ceiling. Her eyes are open but unfocused, showing me that she's here but not really here. *What the hell did they give her?* I'm seconds away from opening my mouth when the blood in my veins freezes. My eyes are glued on the straps that are fastened around her wrists. They fucking tied her to the bed?

"Why is she tied up?" I all but yell at the man that brought me to the room.

"She's very combative, and for our safety and her own, we were advised to strap her down until we could get her to a calm state."

"Calm state? This isn't calm. This is… she's a vegetable."

"I'm sorry, miss, but these are the rules."

"Rules?" I scoff, boiling with rage. I know this is not this guy's fault, but at the moment, he is the one here, and I can't hold in my fury any longer. "How can you do this to an old lady? She would never harm anyone on purpose, she was probably just scared, and you treat her like a prisoner!"

"Ma'am, I need you to calm down—"

"Or what?" I interrupt him. "You'll drug me and tie me to the bed?"

The guy takes a deep breath and I'm surprised by how calm he is. "Look, I know this is not ideal, but we don't have enough staff to have a nurse with your grandma at all hours of the day. This is the option we have to keep her and others safe."

I want to punch the wall, slam the door, and kick the chair. I'm so angry, angry with the situation I'm in, angry with Grams being here, angry with people who don't care about me. But most of all, I'm angry with how helpless I am about all of it.

"Please leave. I want to be alone with her right now." I shoo him away before I can do anything stupid. As badly as I don't want Grams to be here right now, she needs to be.

The nurse frowns before turning and walking out of the room. He closes the door behind him, and I swear I almost burst into tears as soon as the silence of the room engulfs me.

"Grams," I whimper as I cross the room, my hand circling her own. She feels cold to the touch, and I don't like it. I miss having her at home, seeing her smile, listening to her stories. "I miss you so much. It's not the same with you here and me out there."

She doesn't say anything, of course, not like I expected her to, but to hear her voice would be nice. It might calm some of the fear and sadness coursing through me. I unfasten the leather restraints and rub the red skin. Taking the lone seat beside her bed, I grab onto her weathered hand.

"I've missed you. I've even missed your attempts to cook," I half-joke since her last cooking attempt is what landed us here. A long moment of silence settles over us and I bask in it, allowing myself to let go of some of my thoughts, to breathe, to feel. I hate that she's here in this stupid hospital with these stupid nurses.

"I'm sorry I let you down. If I hadn't been job hunting, none of this would've happened. We'd still have a home. You wouldn't be here in this terrible place, and you wouldn't be sedated." Tears prick at my eyes, and I feel the onslaught of emotions threatening to overcome me.

I swipe at my eyes with the back of my hand to stop the tears from staining my cheeks. I don't want her to see me crying when she comes to again. As if she knows how much I need her right now, she stirs against the mattress. Her head moves to the side, and her eyes connect with mine. I'm not sure if she sees me or if she's just looking right through me.

We stay like this for a long time, me just holding her hand, her just looking at me with empty eyes. I wish I could help her, bring her back, and repair her mind.

A knock on the door pulls my attention away from Grams. Before I can say anything, the door creaks open, and a young woman pops her head inside. "Sorry, miss, but visiting hours are nearly over." *Ugh.* That is just my luck.

"Thanks," I mumble beneath my breath, feeling completely defeated.

"Grams," I whisper, and rub my thumb across her hand.

"Stella," she replies, her voice crackly. "Is that you, pumpkin? I missed you so much. I was so sad when a man came to visit me, but you weren't with him."

"Man? What man?" She must be talking about that nurse.

"He asked about you. I can't remember his name right now, but he did ask about you. If I could just remember his name." Her face scrunches up and she gives me a frustrated look.

"It's okay, Grams. Don't worry about it. Just get some rest, okay? I'll come back to visit soon." Hopefully, next time, I'll be taking her with me. She doesn't say anything else, and the light in her eyes dims a little bit, telling me that she's slowly fading back into her mind.

Watching her suffer, seeing her and knowing she doesn't really see me. It hurts so much, far more than I can put into words.

Releasing her hand, I lean in and press a kiss to her cheek and then turn and walk out of the room. Every fiber in my body is trying to stay with her, but I know I can't. I need to go, and I need to find a way to take her with me next time. I know the guys said they would help me, but would they really? And if they do, what will they expect from me in return?

The walk down to the bus stop is short, but it's dark and cold outside now. My thin sweater doesn't give me much protection from the cold. I get my phone out of my jeans pocket just to be reminded about the fact that it's dead. It died right after the nurse called me, and since my charger got fried in the fire, I have no way to charge it. Putting the useless device back, I wrap my arms around myself and keep walking.

With every step I take, the fine hairs on the back of my neck stand up. Paranoid, I look around, waiting for someone to jump out of thin air and attack me, but no one does. I try and shake the thoughts away, but I can't. It feels like someone's eyes are on me, watching my every move. When I reach the bus stop, I shove my hands into the pockets of my sweater and wait impatiently for the bus to show.

I'm looking at the ground, trying to push the image of Grams strapped to that bed out of my mind, when out of nowhere, a hand comes and covers my mouth. In a millisecond, I'm hauled back against a firm chest, the manly smell of soap and pine fills my nostrils as I suck in air through my nose. Before I even have time to panic, he starts talking.

"We told you what would happen if you left," Easton's sinister voice coats my skin in darkness. He sounds angry, more than angry even. He sounds... calm, and if I've learned anything, calm is far worse than crazy. I try and speak against his hand, but the words come out muffled.

"Shut up. I don't want to hear it. We thought we could trust you, and you took that trust and shattered it." Easton's clipped tone is a warning, and I close my mouth, praying for the best while knowing deep down nothing good is going to happen as he walks backward and toward an alleyway.

When he stops, he releases me and opens the door to the blacked-out SUV. He doesn't so much as say a word as he shoves me inside, not so gently. Cam turns in his seat and the look he's giving me, makes me feel so disappointed in myself.

"Grams' nurse called and—" I start but instantly shut up when Easton's hand comes out of nowhere and wraps around my throat. He pulls me across the bench seat, until my face is inches from his own. The feral look in his eyes tells me he wouldn't have a problem strangling me right now. *He's killed once before, what's stopping him from killing you now?*

"I don't care who called you or what they wanted. When we tell you to do something, you fucking do it." He spits the words at me, squeezing a little tighter, making it harder for me to breathe. Anger pours out of him like an infected wound, and I shiver at the coldness of his words. I wheeze as he stares at me, and I stare back at him, not wanting to give up and show weakness. I made a choice, and now I'll take the consequences.

"Let her go, you're hurting her…" Cam orders from the front seat. The softness of his voice slices right through me. They're like night and day, good and bad, but I'm not fooled by it, their end goal is still the same. Keep me silent at all costs.

With a snarl, he releases me and directs his attention to Cam. I sag against the seat, sucking air into my lungs. I've never felt so much anger being directed at me in my life.

"She's your responsibility now. I don't want to fucking deal with her anymore."

For some reason, what he says hits me right in the heart. It almost feels like he's breaking up with me, which is ridiculous since we were never together in the first place. I don't even know what we are. I'm just a piece of meat to them, hanging from the top of the cage. Eventually, they'll jump high enough to reach me and rip me to shreds.

It doesn't matter that they offered to care for Grams and me. They aren't doing it because they care. They're doing it so they can fuck me, and I might be naive, but I'm not stupid enough to believe that they care one more ounce about me outside of that.

"Fine," Cam responds and starts the SUV. We drive in complete silence, Easton ignoring me, putting more and more distance between us as the miles pass.

When we reach the house, I'm shaking, and not just because I'm cold. I'm angry and hurt. Angry with both of them for treating me this way and hurt by the way Easton dismisses me. It's like he decided to be done with me, and that's it. He is throwing me away like a piece of garbage. I should be glad that he's losing interest in me. I should be... that's what my brain is telling me at least, but my stupid heart is getting in the way.

My heart hurts. I feel abandoned and alone, two feelings I know all too well. When I lost my parents, that's all I could feel. I fought many years to be somewhat happy again, to push those feelings down, but today all of them are resurfacing, and I'm not sure if I can find my way back to happiness again.

Easton gets out of the car, slamming the door shut behind him with such force I worry about him breaking something. Cameron gets out as well, opening my door next.

I scurry outside and into the house with Cameron following close behind.

"Are you hungry?"

"No," I whisper, wrapping my arms around my middle a little tighter.

"Let's go take a shower then," he suggests, and I nod my head slightly. He leads me to his bathroom and starts stripping my clothes off, before turning on the water and getting naked himself.

Like everything in this house, the shower is modern, sleek, and expensive looking. There is plenty of room for multiple people, and it even has two showerheads. When the water turns hot enough for it to steam, I step under the spray and let it caress my worn-out body, and my aching muscles.

There is a slight burn between my legs, and I remember what we did just a few hours ago.

"Are you sore?" Cam asks, stepping into the shower.

"A little. It's not bad..." The ache in my chest about what Easton said and how I saw Grams today is much worse. The image of her tied to the bed pops into my mind again, intensifying the pain.

"You look like you're about to cry."

"They tied her to a bed... they gave her drugs and tied her to a bed," I sob, unable to hold my emotions back any longer. Overcome with pain and anger, I seek comfort in the only place I know I can. In Cam's arms. Stepping into him, I bury my face into his chest and snake my arms around his torso.

I think he's going to push me away, but instead, he pulls me closer as I sob against his skin. It's embarrassing and ugly, but I'm like a dam that can't hold any more water. We stand there like that for a while, and he just holds me while I cry in his arms. When I finally compose myself, I stand up straight and wipe the wet strands of hair sticking to my forehead away.

"Don't worry about Grams, I'll take care of that tomorrow. That won't happen again. Now... let me wash you," Cam says his voice soft as he reaches for the soap and a washcloth.

"Okay," I agree, and watch as he soaps the cloth and starts to run it over my body. I can't remember the last time someone took care of me like this. I forgot how nice it felt being cared for, even if this is a one-time deal, I'll gladly take it.

He runs the soapy cloth over my entire body, paying special attention to the tender folds between my legs. When he is done, he washes my hair before rinsing us both off. By the time he's finished, I feel a hundred times better.

"I need to ask you something, and I need you to tell me the truth," he warns as we are stepping out of the shower. His handsome features turn deadly, and I know whatever he has to ask me is important.

"Okay." He grabs a towel from the rack, which I realize is heated when he wraps me in the fluffy cotton.

"Did you tell anybody about that night?" I'm taken aback by his question but answer right away.

"What? No! No, I told you I wouldn't, and I won't." *Why would he think that?* "I just went to see Grams, I swear. I haven't told a single person."

He looks at me for a moment, studying me like he is searching my eyes for a lie, but there is nothing there. "I believe you," he finally says, his eyes softening, "now we just need to make Easton believe you too."

16

EASTON

I give myself twenty-four hours to calm down because if I don't, I'll end up doing something horrible. I'm so enraged with Stella that I all but shoved her into Cameron's arms. Why didn't she just listen to us? Why did she have to go and ruin our fragile bond of trust? I'm stupid, so fucking stupid. I don't know why I'm letting this girl get my emotions tied into a knot. I don't know why I feel so disappointed when I should've expected or seen this coming.

Actually, I do know why, because my stupid fucking heart is getting involved no matter how much I tell that sucker to shut up. I'm getting attached to her, seeing her as a person, and not the fucking thing we need to keep in line to protect ourselves. That's over with now, I'm not letting my feelings get in the way again.

I look up from my phone when I hear a knock on my bedroom door. If that's her, I swear to god, I will lose my fucking mind. A second later, Cameron walks in, and my temper settles a little when I find the blonde-haired siren isn't with him.

Cam doesn't skip a beat as he enters the room, "Look, I know you said you weren't going to watch her, but can you keep an eye on her for like two hours. I have to go make up a test I missed this morning when I took Stella to the doctor."

"Doctor?" I was wondering where they left for this morning.

"Yeah, got her on birth control. Thought you would appreciate that," Cam smiles. "She is on the shot, so we don't have to keep up with her taking the pill."

"Yeah," I grunt, but internally I am excited like a kid on Christmas morning. I didn't pull out like I meant to the other day, but I know I can't keep doing that.

"I also need to go talk to my dad," Cameron explains, "there have been more people coming to the station looking for James. I don't understand how such a cocksucker has people who care about him."

Part of me wants to tell him, no, and the other part knows that I owe it to him to just watch her pain in the ass. He's going to talk to his dad about James, and since someone has to watch her, to keep her from running away or opening her mouth, I guess that lucky person gets to be me.

After a long moment of silence, I say, "Yeah, whatever. I'll watch her, but she better keep her fucking mouth shut." Hearing her voice grates on my every nerve. I want to beg her to keep talking, but also wrap my hand around her throat and shut her up. It's a conundrum I can't explain. The darkness inside of me calls to the goodness in her.

"Perfect. Now, I'm going to warn you, E, if I come home and she's hurt, I'm going to be pissed." *Hurt?*

"You're growing a heart for a girl that doesn't want you. She doesn't want either of us, Cam, and she's using your feelings against you, to make you believe that she does. We still don't know if she is the one who told someone."

Cam rolls his eyes, "It wasn't her who talked, and how I feel about her doesn't matter. I'm asking you not to hurt her." There's a slight plea to his voice, and that only makes me angrier. Stella has weaseled her way under his skin. I'll have to sever that connection today.

"I won't hurt her..." I trail off. *Badly.*

"Don't lie to me," Cam responds, his voice deadpanned, his arms crossed over his chest.

"I'm not lying. I won't hurt her, so long as she keeps her mouth shut and leaves me alone." Cam seems frustrated, but he doesn't say anything else, and before he slips out of the room, I ask, "When are you leaving?"

"Now," he answers, his tone clipped. A short time later, I hear him pulling out of the driveway, so I jump out of bed and leave the room to make sure Stella isn't up to anything she shouldn't be. I check Cam's room first, which is empty before walking out into the living room. As soon as I enter the room, I see her sitting there on the sectional, staring out the window. I have half a second before she notices me, but that half-second of staring at her is enough to make my heart beat out of my chest.

Our gazes collide, and angry fire ripples through my veins. I hate how she makes me feel. I hate that she has this power over me. Breaking the moment between us, I turn around and walk into the kitchen. Heading for the cabinet, I pull out a glass and place it on the counter, before moving toward the fridge.

"Cam said not to talk to you, but..."

"Obviously, you have a hard time listening," I growl. Her voice does something to me. It awakens the beast, it makes me crave her, it makes me want to possess and mark every inch of her flesh. Like she's mine.

Her bare feet pad against the floor, and I can hear her moving behind me. She should know never to corner a monster. Never to try and reason with the unreasonable.

"I didn't mean to disobey. I just wanted to see..." The sound of nails on a chalkboard fills my ears, and I grab the glass I placed on the counter and smash it on the floor, wanting to make the noise disappear, wanting to make her shut up.

"I don't care what your excuse was. You broke our fucking trust," I yell, my throat throbbing as the words push from it.

Stella's angelic face turns stoic, and I can see the fear trickling into her features like a leak in the ceiling. *Drip by slow drip.* I'm vibrating with anger, trying to figure out what the fuck I'm going to do next when she drops down to her knees and starts to pick up the broken pieces of glass.

What the fuck?

"What are you doing?"

Looking up at me through thick lashes, she says, "Picking up the broken glass."

I don't know why but I snap and tug her up off the floor by her arm. She gasps and then winces as the pieces of glass in her hand fall back to the floor, shattering into even tinier pieces. Grabbing her by the hips, I place her ass on the edge of the counter. I'm not gentle as I do so either, and I know she'll probably have bruises where I've touched her, but I can't bother to be gentle with her, not when I want to shake her, rip out her perfectly, sweet heart.

In this position, we're eye level with each other, and as she looks at me with both fear and desire in her eyes, I grapple with my need to either destroy or claim her. She's ruined me, claimed a part of me that I've never given to anyone else, and she's done so without even knowing it. As I look down her body, ready to rip her clothes off and ravage her, my eyes catch on something red. *Blood.* Her finger is bleeding and all because she tried to make herself the heroine by picking up the broken pieces of glass.

"It's just a tiny cut," she murmurs, her gaze dropping down to her hand. I grab onto the finger and bring it to my lips. The blood beads against the tip of her finger, it's a tiny cut, much smaller than the one she's inflicted upon me with her betrayal.

"Yesterday, you destroyed my trust in you. Today, you find a way to earn it back."

"I didn't mean to..." She starts but I cut her off by wrapping my other hand around her throat. If the darkness in my eyes doesn't shut her up, that certainly will. I rub her finger over my bottom lip. The warmth of her blood on my skin teases the beast that lingers just beneath the surface. Our gazes collide, we're fire and gasoline, and as soon as we touch, we'll blow up the entire fucking world.

Letting my tongue dart out over my bottom lip, I lick the coppery tang away. The taste of her blood excites me, and my barely-there resolve shatters. In a second, I have her over my shoulder as I walk us toward my bedroom.

Once over the threshold, I toss her down on the bed and start ripping her clothes off.

"Make me forgive you... prove to me that I can trust you."

"What do you want from me?" she croaks, and there's a fragileness to her voice that I'm drawn too.

"Everything," I snarl, "your body, your heart, your dreams, and your fears. Everything you hold dear... I want it. I want every single piece of you." I slide my palm down her chest, and cup her by one breast. She shivers but doesn't flinch away from me. I smile like the devil before I pinch the nipple of that same breast, watching as her face morphs with pleasure.

"Easton..." She says my name like it's a prayer, and I'm her maker, but I'm no god. I'm the devil, a ruthless, selfish bastard, and right now, all I want to do is consume her.

Stripping out of my own clothes, I pounce on her, spreading her thighs so I can feast my eyes on her pink pussy. She's dripping with arousal, and I'm ready to explode, so I flip her onto her stomach and watch as she slowly moves onto her hands and knees.

"I'm going to fuck you now. Fuck you so hard you'll feel me for days, and then I'm going to come inside of you. You want that?"

"Yes," she says breathlessly.

"But, there's a catch... you don't get to come, you have to earn that from me. You have to make me want to give you a release." Disappointment flickers in her eyes as she looks at me over her shoulder.

She's trusting me, but we all know she shouldn't. I'm the most unstable person out of the three of us, but I guess we'll find out if

Cameron made a mistake leaving me alone with this little bird or not.

With bruising force, I take her by the hips and guide my cock to her center. I grit my teeth as I slam balls deep inside of her, relishing in the pleasure that zings down my cock and into my veins. I've never had such perfect pussy in my life.

Like a sex-crazed siren, Stella arches her head back and lets out a soft feminine moan. I try and ignore the sound, but it's like a beacon of light in my complete dark mind, and I want to let myself be touched by her. I want to know what it's like to be possessed, to be wanted. Blocking out the thought before it can take root, I pull out and slam back in. My thrust is so hard, Stella loses her balance and falls onto her face.

She twists, so her face isn't completely buried in the mattress and pushes her ass out, driving my cock deeper into her precious pussy. Black spots appear in my vision as I fuck her with a ferociousness that borders the mentally insane. I want to embed myself beneath her skin, to feel her heartbeat within my own. If this is what love feels like, then I want to experience it again and again until my very last breath.

I feel the distinct flutter of her pussy telling me that she's close to coming, but that's not going to happen today.

"Don't come," I growl, and she mewls into the mattress, letting me use her body. I rut harder and faster until I'm sure I'm breaking her in two. Then with a roar, I explode, filling her pussy with every last drop of come that's in my balls. I'm completely spent when I pull out of her, and with my heart beating out of my chest, I sag down to the mattress beside her.

We're both breathing heavy, while locks of Stella's blonde hair stick to her clammy forehead. Tears pool in her eyes, and that fucking look she's giving me, hits me right in the stomach. I don't know what it is about her, but I'm weak, so fucking weak for her.

"I told you that you didn't get to come," I huff out.

"I know, but please, I need to... I need you to make me forget."

"Forget what?"

"Everything... my life and everything that has been going wrong. I want to forget all of it, just for a little while."

She is so vulnerable in this moment, her guard is down, and I know she will tell me things now she usually wouldn't. "Tell me. Tell me what you feel like right now and what you need."

"I feel like a doll. Like some sex doll you just use to come inside of. Don't leave me like this... I need you. I need you to make me feel better." The tears start to fall, and I'm overcome with the possessive need to make her pain go away.

"Roll over and spread your legs." Immediately, she does as I say. Her thighs fall apart, and I sit up. "Like I said, you can earn my trust back. See, trust goes both ways. Show me that you trust me, so I can trust you again."

"I do," she pants, and even though I know she would say anything in her lust-stricken mind right now, I'll take it. Getting up from the bed, I get a set of handcuffs from my dresser. As soon as she sees the shiny object in my hand, her eyes go wide. They gleam with both curiosity and a sniggle of fear.

"I'm gonna cuff you to my bed, and you're gonna let me do whatever I want with you." Her breath hitches at my words, but she nods her head slightly.

Looping the handcuffs around my bedpost, I grab her wrists and cuff them together. Looking down at her naked body, stretched out and tied up on my bed, has my dick hard again. Fuck, why didn't I tie her up before?

Getting back on the bed, I move between her legs. Her pussy is swollen and dripping with come, my come. Satisfaction, like I've never felt before, fills my chest.

"Please. Please, make me come. Don't tease me, Easton. I'm sorry for what I did. I promise it wasn't intentional. I didn't betray you." I know she means every word she says, and it's then that I choose to let go of my anger toward her. I want her too much to hold onto that anger.

With two fingers, I enter her swollen cunt, my cock hardening as I feel her muscles flutter and tense around my fingers. Using my other hand, I trail it up her stomach and then her chest, wrapping my fingers around her throat once I reach it. She peers up at me, so innocently, it almost fractures a piece of my black heart.

She lifts her hips and bites her bottom lip as pleasure threatens to swallow her whole. The handcuffs clink together as she tugs on them. Her whole body squirming beneath my touch as she falls off the cliff's edge, my fingers continue moving in and out of her come-filled pussy.

"I'm coming..." She sighs, confirming what I already knew. Her eyes fall closed, and she shudders and gushes her release on my hand and the sheets. All I can do is smile at the feeling that giving her pleasure brings me. With my fingers wrapped around her throat, I give her a gentle squeeze, forcing her eyes to open.

"Leave us again, and I'll kill you myself..." I growl, staring deeply into her gray eyes. Gray eyes that have ensnared my black heart. She nods her head in understanding, and I release her. Grabbing the key from the nightstand, I uncuff her quickly. She tugs her hands down and turns onto her side with her eyes closed.

Moving away from the bed. I stare down at her, and all I can think is mine.

All. Fucking. Mine.

∼

AFTER CLEANING HER UP, Stella falls asleep on the bed. I pull the blanket up and over her body, so she doesn't get cold before I pull on a pair of boxers and walk out into the kitchen. I find the broom and dustpan and sweep up the broken glass from the kitchen floor. God knows if Cameron walks in the door right now, he'll think the worst.

Finished with cleaning up, I make sure there aren't any pieces of glass that linger and then pop a pizza into the oven for Stella and me. Just as I'm pulling it out of the oven, Cam walks through the door. He eyes me cautiously, taking note of my nearly naked body, and it's obvious who he is looking for.

"Where is she?"

"Handcuffed to the bed," I grin.

"Easton," he growls, "you promised you wouldn't hurt her." He heads toward my bedroom, and I follow behind him.

"I didn't, and I was kidding. I uncuffed her before leaving the room," I say as he pushes the door open. His gaze widens when he finds Stella completely tanked, snoring happily against the sheets.

"You fucked her?" He turns to me, a slight grin on his lips.

"I sure did, and I feel ten times better. I should have just fucked her yesterday, would have saved me a sleepless night."

"You should have, but your head got in the way. Glad you finally came to your senses."

"I don't know if this is having sense. I feel like the opposite like I've lost my mind. I can't really explain it, but she's got this hold on me. She makes me feel, and I can't let her go. I just can't." Cameron nods his head, and I know he understands. Every day that we surround ourselves with her is another day that we fall deeper into our feelings.

"Do you think it's possible to love something that was never meant to be yours?" Cam asks as he pulls the door closed.

"You're wrong. She was always meant to be ours, that much is true."

17

STELLA

The tension between Easton and I seeps away, and I feel closer to both guys, closer than I've ever felt. My feelings for them are still hard to digest, and Easton's confession to me the other day has made them even harder to sink in. Being with them is wrong, but it also feels completely right.

"*Leave us again, and I'll kill you myself...*" The words haunt me like a never-ending nightmare. Would he do it? Part of me believes he would since I know how insane he is, but part of me questions his ability to let go of his feelings for me. I know he cares about me. I know our connection is deeper, so I know it wouldn't be that easy for him to give me up or shut off his emotions. He wants me to believe that he doesn't want me, but I know better. I might be naive, but I'm not stupid.

With Easton at class, Cameron and I have the entire house to ourselves. We spend most of the morning in bed, cuddling, which is a nice change. Having two men care for you is the best of both worlds. One is kind, sweet, and completely swoonworthy, while the other makes your pulse pound. Easton is demanding, possessive, and alpha as fuck. Where Cam gives, Easton takes, and I'm simply stuck in the middle of their insane push and pull.

"What are you thinking about?" Cam asks as he traces his fingers over my skin. It's nearly one, and I haven't managed to do a single thing today. It's nice, but I feel guilty because I'm here enjoying a day of peace while Grams is still in that damn hospital.

I consider lying to him, but I know he'll know if I lie. There's this strange connection between the three of us, and sometimes I think they know me better than I know myself.

"Grams. I miss her," I reply honestly.

"It's been a couple of days since you saw her last, maybe you should go and visit her?" I pull away to look at his face, just to make sure I'm hearing him clearly.

"Did you just offer to let me leave?" I can't stop my lips from turning up into a grin.

"Believe it or not, I do trust you. I believed you when you told me you only left to help Grams. I'm not Easton. I'm possessive, and you're mine, but I don't want to dull out your light or break you, Stella."

And Easton does? I want to ask but don't.

"Are you sure he won't get mad that you let me leave? You're a team."

Cam's face turns serious, and he cups me by the cheek, his touch so gentle, it's almost strange to want that kindness.

"Make no mistake of who we are together. We make decisions as a team, and we share you completely in every way. Easton's opinion matters, but letting you see your grams isn't going to hurt us. You haven't told anyone or caused any real trouble, so you deserve a reward. This is my gift to you."

Without thinking, I lean into him and press my lips against his firm full ones. His eyes light up, and he seems just as shocked by the kiss as I am. I've never gone out of my way to kiss either of them, but as my feelings change, my need for them deepens. I never used to need their touch, their words, or to be possessed by them, but now it feels like a part of me dies when they aren't there.

"Thank you," I whisper against his lips as I pull away.

"You're welcome, now leave before I change my mind and take you into my bed and ravage you until neither of us can do anything but breathe."

The thought sends goosebumps across my skin but seeing Grams outweighs my ever-growing arousal. I dig through the box of clothes Easton had someone bring for me. He said her name is Willow and that she goes to school with the guys. I can't help but wonder if that's the same Willow I met in the cafeteria.

He emphasized her not being one of his ex-girlfriends, which, of course, was my first thought. All the clothes in here are very nice and very expensive looking, which I am definitely not used to, but I won't lie and say I'm not excited about wearing them.

"We'll take you shopping this weekend so you can pick out your own clothes," Cameron says from the bed, watching me get dressed.

"This is like the nicest stuff I've ever worn, so I am perfectly fine with these," I admit and motion to the box. Cam's smile fades a little bit, almost like he is sad for me. What he doesn't understand is that I never really cared about having money for clothes, all I wanted was for Grams to be safe and happy.

I move away from him and head for the foyer. I've only made it a couple feet when he comes up behind me.

"Be back by eight, and I mean it. I don't want to have to go out and find you, and you definitely don't want Easton to have to find you." He winks, but the thought makes me shiver.

"Got it," I reply, the heaviness in my chest lifting a little. Cameron is giving me a slice of freedom, and I won't let him down. I'll be good.

With a kiss to the forehead, he lets me leave, and I all but skip from the house. I take the short bus ride to the hospital downtown, my new jacket keeping me warm as I walk from the bus to the hospital entrance.

Just like last time, I wait up front for someone to come and get me. When the same guy from last time greets me, I can't help but frown, even though he smiles.

"Good to see you, your grandma is doing so much better now," he explains, and my mood brightens up in seconds.

"She is?" I ask, almost scared he is just being a sarcastic asshole.

"Yes, follow me. She has been asking about you non-stop." He leads me to the closed wing, and I follow eagerly. We head the same way as last time, but when we get to the room Grams was in, he continues walking.

"She got moved," he explains before I can ask the question out loud.

"Where to?"

"A nicer room," is all he offers in response. My heart skips a beat, Cameron kept his word, he must have done something to have her moved.

We turn the corner and walk through another door into a different corridor, and immediately I notice the difference between the two halls. The walls are painted a nice pastel color instead of the dreadful hospital white. There are pictures hanging on the walls, and even the doors and floors are nicer. In fact, the place feels and starts to look more homey.

"Right here, this one," he stops and opens a door for me, and as soon as I stick my head inside, I see Grams. She is sitting on a rocking chair by the window, knitting something. She looks up at me, and her whole face lights up. Instantly, I'm reminded of home, of how things used to be, and I wish I could turn back the clock and be there that day, instead of out job searching.

"Stella, there you are." She smiles widely.

I all but run to her, closing the distance between us in three long strides. Wrapping my arms around her, I bury my face into the crook of her neck. Even in this place, her scent hasn't changed. She still smells like lilacs, like *my* Grams. Her slender arms come around me, and she pats me gently on the back. When I pull away, I study her face to see if she's fully here this time.

"I missed you, Grams," I tell her wholeheartedly.

"No reason to miss me, child. I'm right here," she smiles, all the heartache from last time I was here forgotten. The image of Grams tied to the bed is banished from my mind for good. I refuse to think about her in that situation.

We spend the next hour simply sitting together, enjoying each other's company. We talk a little, but most of the time, I just watch her knit. It seems to be therapeutic for both of us. I'm so relaxed and zoned out I almost don't notice when my phone starts buzzing in my pocket.

I pull it out and read the text that appears on the screen.

Katie: Want to meet up for coffee and catch up?

Staring at the screen for a long second, I contemplated my response. The idea of hanging out with someone other than Easton, Cam, or even Grams is tempting. I haven't had a friend to talk to in a long time, and god knows I could use one now.

My fingers hover over the buttons as I imagine myself typing out a yes response. Cam and Easton wouldn't mind, would they? It's just coffee, and we are over the whole trust issue, right?

"What's eating you?" Grams asks out of nowhere, not even looking up from her knitting.

"Oh, nothing, just worried about you. I'm sorry I haven't been able to visit much."

"You can stay, sweetie, you don't have to go to school today, right?" Once again, I'm reminded that Grams is still lost in the past, and I'll never be able to reach her there. I'm moving forward, and she's forever stuck in the past.

"I have to go, but I'll be back soon. I promise." Grams doesn't even frown, in fact, she smiles. Before I give her a hug, I type out a response to Katie, asking if she wants to meet up at the coffee place around the corner.

Giving Grams a hug, I shove my phone back into my pocket and give her a tiny wave. As I walk out of the hospital, I realize that for the first time in a long time, I don't feel guilty leaving Grams alone. Because she isn't alone. She is taken care of now, and that alone is a huge burden off my chest. I hate thinking about it that way because she isn't supposed to be a burden, and she isn't.

It's just the responsibility that always weighs down on me. The need to keep her safe, the worry that something might happen to her because I wasn't there. This feeling is absent now, and I know who I have to thank for that. Thinking about them, I know I have to make sure they know where I am. Pulling out my phone, I pull up Cam's number and send him a text telling him where I'm going and that I am still going to be home at eight as promised.

I walk into the coffee shop and get in line at the counter. Overwhelmed by the oversized menu, I'm not sure what to order, so I end up getting a coffee with cream and sugar. I dig around my wallet to find my emergency five dollar bill stuffed behind my ID. I usually don't touch that unless it's a true emergency, but lately, I'm in a constant state of emergency anyway, so I think a coffee will be just fine.

As I'm sitting down at a table near the window, Katie walks in. She waves at me and gets her own drink at the counter before coming to sit by me.

"Hey, girl, I've been worried about you," is the first thing out of her mouth. I try and hide my puzzled expression from her.

"Hey. Why have you been worried?" I ask as she settles into the seat across from me.

She shrugs. "You left so suddenly the other night, and we didn't hear from you again. Plus, you left with Cameron and Easton, and those two are known to be trouble."

"Oh, really?" I pretend like I don't have a clue what she's talking about. "As you can see, I'm fine. Sorry to have worried you."

"Are you still staying in that motel?"

"No... I'm staying... uhhh, somewhere else now."

Katie nods, and purses her lips, "As long as it's not with Cameron and Easton, I'll be happy for you."

A mixture of jealousy and anger swirls around in my stomach. Jealousy because Katie knows them, and I'm guessing it's from the strip club and anger because of the way she talks about them. In my head, I know she is right, Cam and Easton are trouble, big huge trouble. Still, I know she's just being a good friend and watching out for me, but I can't help but feel protective about them, which is ridiculous if I think about it.

"So, where are you staying now?" She questions, and for some reason, it feels like I'm being interrogated. Why does she care so much about where I'm staying? Or if I'm hanging out with Cameron and Easton. It's none of her business.

"Oh no, you are staying with them." Horror fills her features.

"I am," I admit, feeling ashamed, even though I shouldn't. I don't owe her an excuse.

"Why? How do you even know them?" My mouth pops open at her question. Crap, what am I going to tell her? I watched them kill someone in the alley behind the cafeteria? Somehow, I don't think that's going to fly.

"She used to work on campus," a familiar voice interrupts, making my head snap up. My tongue feels heavy in my mouth when I see that Cameron is standing behind me, an angry scowl painted on his handsome face. Right now, he looks like the devil, and I'm seconds away from being banished to hell.

"Oh, hey, Cam," Katie smiles, fakeness oozing from every pore on her body. "Are you going to join us for a coffee?"

"No, thanks. We're leaving, *now*." His words are clipped, and I don't understand why he is so mad. I told him where I was going. Granted, I didn't tell him who I was seeing, I don't think that matters, so long as I'm not with any other men. "Come on, Stella." He grabs me by the arm and pulls me up and onto my feet.

Confusion morphs into anger, and I feel like a small child being scolded. I chew the inside of my cheek to stop myself from lashing out. Without saying another word, he drags me out of the coffee shop and down the sidewalk.

The wind whips through my hair, and I dig my feet into the concrete in an effort to slow him down. I've never seen him so angry. His grasp tightens, and I wince, my wrist throbbing where he holds it.

"I didn't do anything," I growl once we finally reach the car. I'm still shocked to see him so angry. I don't understand what I've done, and I'm tired of being quiet.

"Right now, would be a good fucking time for you to keep your mouth shut." His tone of voice is frightening as he releases me and opens the door. His brown eyes which are usually filled with mischief or joy brim with burning rage.

Why is he so mad?

I want to push him, beg him to tell me why, but I'm afraid that if I stick my neck out on the chopping block, he'll cut it off.

"Get in the car, Stella, because if I have to put you in it, it isn't going to be a good experience for you." Impatience drips from his lips, and against my better judgment, I climb into the car. I mean, where the hell would I go anyway? How would I pay for Grams to stay in the hospital? It's a lose, lose situation for me. I was damned from the very beginning.

The entire drive home Cam white knuckles the steering wheel, his impeccable jaw is clenched so tight, I can practically see his control slipping. I huddle against the door of the car, anger, and fear pumping through my veins at an accelerated rate. It feels like I'm on the edge of a cliff, hanging on by the tips of my fingers.

We drive in silence until we pull up to the house. When I see Easton's car in the driveway, I start to get really worried. If Cam is this mad, how mad is Easton going to be? A knot forms in my stomach, and my throat closes up, making it hard to swallow.

"Just tell me why you're so mad," I whisper, but Cam just gets out of the car without a word. I take a deep breath before getting out of the car myself and follow him inside. I'm scared of what's to come, it's like looking into dark waters and knowing a shark is lurking beneath the surface, but you just don't know where.

Neither of them has ever physically hurt me, but I'm starting to wonder how much longer this can all go on before they do. As soon as we make it through the front door, Easton appears in the doorway of the living room.

"What the fuck were you thinking?" he yells, his voice booming through the hallway, causing me to jump.

"I was just getting a coffee. I don't understand why you guys are so mad. Cam said I could go as long as I was back at eight. It's only seven-thirty."

"I said you could go see Grams!" Cam yells from beside me, his body twitching, probably because he wants to kill me.

"And I did, but then Katie asked me to meet up for coffee, and I didn't think it would be a big deal," I stand up for myself. "I texted you—"

"Did you tell her anything?" Easton cuts me off, his gaze narrowing.

"What? No... I would never. It was just coffee..."

"I told you letting her go was a mistake." Easton shoves a hand through his hair, frustration bubbling out of him. Something inside of me snaps, and I take a step back and shake my head at both of them.

"*Letting* me go?" I question, finally losing it. I've had enough, I can't let them treat me like this any longer. "I'm not a thing or a prisoner, and I'm not with either of you. I'm not dating you guys. I'm just here, living in this stupid house with two psychotic men, who I witnessed kill someone. I'm tired of being treated like shit. I'm tired of being talked down to," I yell, "I'm a human, and I'm allowed to visit my grandma and have coffee with a friend if I want to."

Easton blinks. I watch as shock slowly appears in his eyes before it morphs into pure blind rage. Dread curls in my gut, and I know that I've made a mistake. No doubt about it, I'm going to regret saying what I did by the end of the night.

He closes the distance between us with superhuman speed. I barely have time to gasp in shock as he grabs me and hauls me over his shoulder. His touch is bruising as he walks to the bedroom and tosses me onto the bed. I bounce against the mattress once before scrambling backward toward the headboard.

"If you're going to hurt me, just do it already. I'm tired of being trapped here. Tired of feeling like I'm going insane." Tears sting my eyes, but I blink them away. I will not give him the satisfaction of seeing me cry.

"You think you're trapped?" Easton tilts his head to the side, and I can tell the moment the switch inside his head flips. The Easton I know is gone; this is a side of him that I've never seen before.

18

CAMERON

Fire burns in her gray eyes, and I swear my cock grows as hard as steel. There is something about her, something that I don't understand. It's like she wants us to hurt her. She tempts us, provoking the beasts inside of us. She knows how dangerous we are, how evil we are, and yet she pushes us until we're at our limits.

"I don't *think* I'm trapped; I know I am," she replies defiantly. Easton's already seething, and if she doesn't watch herself, she'll be in for a world of hurt. Even though I'm angry, I'm not as short-tempered as him. "I'm tired of being treated like crap, like a slave to your needs." Her lip curls with anger, and I want to bite it. Taste her anger on my tongue.

Easton glares at me over his shoulder, and I know what he wants. He wants to subdue her, show her just how vile we can be. I also know that he's looking for my permission, he wants to make sure that I am with him on this. Unfortunately for Stella, I am.

Giving him a slight nod, I watch as the corner of his mouth tucks upward, forming a diabolical smirk.

"You know what I think?" Easton asks in a low tone, "I think we've been treating you too well. We've been giving you too much freedom.

I don't think we've been treating you like a slave, but maybe we should. Maybe that's exactly what you want or better yet *need*?"

Even from across the room, I can see Stella shaking on the bed. Her back is against the headboard, and her legs are pulled up to her chest. Her body language tells me she is scared, but when I look into her steel-gray eyes, I can see something more hiding right beneath the surface... desire. She wants this, but she's just too damned ashamed and afraid to admit it. Lucky for her, we know her body better than even she does.

"I think you are right, Easton. This might be exactly what she needs."

"No," Stella whimpers like a wounded animal as she scoots closer to the headboard, pressing her back against it like she can get away from us. It's too late for that now, there is no escaping us anymore, maybe there never was.

Walking around the bed, her eyes jump between Easton and me. He gets a pair of handcuffs from his drawer while I stalk around the bed like a predator. There was only one other time Stella has seen me like this, and that's the first night we met. Up until this point, I've never had a reason to show this side of myself.

When I'm right beside the bed, her eyes lock on mine, and I know she sees it too.

Fear overcomes her, and she tries to make a run for it. Leaping off the bed, she tries to get past me, but I'm much quicker than her. Easton is by our side the next instant, and together, we start taking her clothing off. Her arms are flailing, and her legs are kicking as she tries to fight us, but we overcome her with ease.

Grabbing her arms, I pull them behind her back, and Easton slaps the handcuffs on her wrists. When she is completely naked and even more helpless than before, I drop her on the bed face first so we can take our own clothes off.

"I hate you," she mumbles into the mattress, attempting to crawl away. Tossing my shirt to the floor, I land a hard slap to her bare ass. A gasp of pleasure slips past her lips.

"No, you don't," Easton answers. "And maybe that's the problem. Maybe we need to give you a real reason to feel that way."

Both naked now, we crawl onto the bed. Stella tries to wiggle away, but I grab her ankle and pull her back toward me. Easton grabs her other ankle and does the same, spreading her wide as he does.

"Of course, you're wet," I say when I see her arousal glistening on the folds of her pussy.

Easton is already holding the lube in his hand. Opening the top, he squirts a good amount on her ass cheek before closing the cap and tossing the container away. Using my free hand, I rub the liquid into her skin, moving between her legs as I do. I leave my thumb pressed against her tight asshole, massaging it, but like the lioness that she is, she fights us, doing her best to keep her legs closed.

"You better relax that ass for us, or this is going to really hurt," I tell her just as I push my thumb inside, forcing the tight ring of muscles to give way. She groans and arches her back into my touch while I push my thumb deeper and deeper. I pump it in and out a few times, before pulling away and replacing it with two fingers. I stretch her, preparing her for Easton's cock.

Easton and I both watch as her ass swallows my fingers beautifully. The lube making them slide in and out with ease.

"I think she's ready," Easton says, sounding every bit as impatient as I am right now. He lies down next to her on the mattress, and motions for me to hand her to him. Grabbing her hips, I hoist her up and flip her around, so she is facing me.

"What are you doing?" she asks, her eyes wide and brimming with lust, and all I can do is smile. She fights us so hard, and yet here she is, panting with need for our cocks.

"Fucking you," I tell her as I place her on Easton's chest. He grabs her hips and lines himself up with her ass. Pre-come beads at the tip of my cock as I watch Easton sink himself into her tight little asshole inch by inch.

Her head falls back against his chest, and her tits push out as she slowly leans back. With her hands cuffed behind her back, Easton's dick in her ass, and her legs spread out for me, she looks like the most delicious buffet I've ever seen... and I'm a starving man.

It's time for me to take my share.

"Tell me you want me in your pussy? Tell me that you want both of us to fuck you together. That you need both cocks," I order and pinch her chin between two fingers. Her pink lips part, and her tongue darts out. Easton thrusts deep in her ass, and I know it's hard for her to focus, but she isn't getting my dick until she admits she wants both of us.

I stroke my own cock, looking down at her glistening pussy that's begging for me to fuck it before directing my attention back to her face. "Say it, Stella...

"I want your cock..."

"And?" I grin. "Where do you want it?"

She starts to pant, her eyes heavy with pleasure, "In my pussy..."

"Say you want both our cocks, and I'll reward you with a long hard fuck."

"Yes," she groans, "I want both of your cocks. Please..." I release her chin and smile with satisfaction as I move between her legs. Sliding my cock through her folds, I gather her arousal against the head of my cock before I push into her tight channel slowly. My mouth waters as I watch her pussy swallow the head of my cock. If I didn't believe it before, I do now. She was made for us.

Having Easton in her ass makes her pussy even tighter, so tight it's hard to gain entry, but I still do. I thrust deep until every inch of my cock is inside of her, and her face is scrunched up into an expression that mirrors both pain and pleasure.

"So full," she mutters, her eyes squeezed shut. Her body is tense, and I know I need her to relax before I can really start fucking her.

She's squeezing me so tight, I can barely breathe. My balls tighten, and if I really wanted to, I could come right now, but I'm not selfish. If anyone gets to come first, it's going to be Stella.

Running my hands up and over her chest, I gently stroke her breasts before cupping one in my hand. So soft and perfect. I pinch the dusky pink tip between my fingers and then roll it alternating between bites of pain and pleasure. Easton brushes the thick mane of blonde hair away from her neck and peppers kisses against her tender skin there. I can basically see her melting between us, her body like a chocolate bar. Finally, she's giving herself over to the sensations, accepting us into her body.

"That's it, relax," I coo, as I pick up speed. With every thrust, I edge closer to heaven, knowing that when I come, I'm gonna come so hard I'll see stars. Fuck, she feels so good, too good. No way should sex feel this good between us. At a punishing pace, we work her body, it doesn't take long for her to start falling apart.

"I'm coming…" She whimpers as her eyes flutter closed, and her body ripples with pleasure, her pussy clenching around my cock.

"Fuck," I growl.

"Jesus fucking Christ…" Easton grunts as he forces his cock into her ass. "Do that again, and I'm going to explode in your ass," he confesses, pain lacing his words, and I get it. I want to go off like a rocket right now, but I also want her to come again.

Moving a hand between our bodies, I stroke her diamond hard clit, feeling her release drip down my balls.

"You want our come inside you, don't you?"

"Yes," she whimpers, her eyes hazy with post-orgasmic pleasure.

"Good… I need you to come again. Fall apart all over my cock, show me how much you want both of us. Let us fill you with our come until it's dripping out of you. Until you're nothing but a melty mess of come, tears, and pleasure."

"Oh…" Her mouth forms an O, and her eyes go wide as I rub my cock against the soft tissue at the top of her pussy. "It… it hurts… I can't…" She grimaces, and I know we're pushing her to her limits, but I'm not stopping until she comes again. I'll fuck her all day if I have to.

"You can, and you will." I harden my words and pinch her clit hard, "Make that pussy gush, come, now!" I order and watch as the pleasure encompasses her.

"Oh, god. Oh, god…" She starts to come then, her pussy clenching me so hard my eyes roll to the back of my head. I thrust harder and deeper and start to come too.

"Shit, shit… I'm coming," Easton roars as he thrusts faster and faster.

I clench my jaw and let the pleasure slam into me, wave after wave crashes against me as I empty every drop of my release into her tight cunt.

Entirely spent, my cock softens, and I slip out of her, watching as a mixture of her release and my own drip out of her pussy.

"You belong to us, and if you didn't believe it before, you better now. There is nothing you can do to escape us, nothing you can do to get away. You like what we do to you, you like that we use your body, and fuck you savagely, and that's okay. We're all a little fucked up, and that's okay because the best people are a little bit broken."

Easton pulls out of her gently, after emptying himself inside her ass, and my cock starts to harden all over again at the image of both of her holes dripping with sticky white come. E rolls her over onto her side and moves off the bed.

"Will you uncuff me now?" she questions, her eyes heavy. I look to Easton, and I can tell he wants to keep her like this, to teach her a lesson and as soft as I am for her, I know she needs this lesson. She needs to see that we've been treating her well, because maybe then she'll appreciate us more.

"No, you'll stay like this until we see fit," Easton tells her. Her eyes widen in shock, and she looks up at me like she expects me to say something, but I just shake my head at her.

Both of us get dressed and walk out of the room, leaving her just like that, filled with our come, and consumed with pleasure.

∼

AN HOUR LATER, I walk into Easton's room and find Stella asleep, still lying on her side. It's been hard as fuck leaving her in here, but I've managed by keeping myself busy. As if she's a lighthouse on a dark, deserted beach, I am drawn to her. Crawling up onto the bed, I sit beside her and trace my fingers over her delicate skin.

She called herself our doll, our slave, but we don't just want her around for sex. We want her around for everything. We want to fuck her, yes, but we also enjoy controlling her, owning her in a way. She's so much more than just some girl we screw, she's definitely nothing like any other girl before her. Moving my hand down, I find our come dry against her skin.

Her pink pussy taunts me, and I move a finger between her folds, finding her little clit. I rub gentle circles against the nub until Stella starts to wake up. Then I move lower, pressing two fingers into her entrance. Tight like a glove, she squeezes my fingers as soon as I enter.

"Mmmm," she mewls into the mattress.

"Mmmm, is right. Tell me who owns this pussy," I order, pumping in and out of her.

"You," she croaks, her voice sleepy and her eyes still closed. "You and Easton. Both of you."

"Who gives you pleasure?" I move faster, taking note of her heavy breathing. She rolls over then and spreads her legs wide, giving me a perfect view.

"You," she whimpers, opening her eyes, she begs me for a release with them. Curling my fingers upward, I rub against her g-spot and watch as she erupts, and pleasure blooms in her features. As she floats down, I remove my fingers and gently stroke her folds.

"Are you going to let me go now?" she whispers.

I shake my head, "No. You accused us of treating you like a slave, so we're going to show you what that really feels like. From today forward, you're going to be our good little sex doll, and let us use you because that's all you think you are to us."

Her eyes water and I can tell she's fighting back tears, "That's not what I meant, and you both know it. I'm just tired of being treated like I'm nothing to both of you. I want to be..." she pauses, probably trying to find the right words. "I don't know, I just don't want to be treated like a child. I want to be your equals." My jaw hardens, and I stare at her for a long second. I understand what she's saying, but I don't know how to handle it.

Having her be our equal would mean that we'd have to give up control over her. For that, we would have to trust each other deeply, and I don't think we are there yet. We can't put what happened behind us, it's too soon.

"Please, Cameron," she pleads with me, her voice sounding small.

"I will see what Easton wants to do, but for right now, this is how it's going to be." My chest aches when I see the hope in her eyes diminish, and her eyes fill with more tears. Pulling the blanket over her naked body, I cover her up as she curls into herself again.

Neither of us want to really hurt her, but we're all walking a fine line, and we will all either end up on one side or the other.

The question is, will it be the side where she becomes ours or the one where we have no choice but to let her go.

19

STELLA

I spend the next day sulking and licking my wounds, while the guys treat me like a child that needs to be supervised. They didn't leave me cuffed for long, thank god, but I might as well be on a leash. The only time I'm allowed to be alone is to use the bathroom.

Mostly, I have been bored because Cam and Easton had to do school work, and they wouldn't even let me help, which enrages me even more. Do they think I'm stupid? The only reason I'm not in college is money and the fact that I had Grams to care for. I could have easily gotten an academic scholarship.

At least, now something is happening, even though I don't know if this is a good or a bad thing. Cameron keeps me locked in his bedroom, while what I can only describe as a complete mass explosion takes place inside the house.

"She fucking left, she just left," a deep scary voice yells. The sound vibrates through the walls of the house, followed by something shattering against the floor. What the hell are they doing? It sounds like they are tearing this entire place apart.

"She's a bitch, Warren. You never should've let her back into your life," Easton yells back, the deep gravelly sound resonating through me.

"Shut the fuck up!" Warren snarls, and I look to Cameron, who doesn't seem phased by the events that are taking place just outside the room.

"Warren can be a little intense sometimes," he mumbles, pulling me into his side. Even though I know Easton can hold his own, I'm still worried that something is going to happen to him. I don't say anything, and instead, listen as the sounds outside the room die down.

Staring at the bedroom door, I wait for Easton to appear.

"Worried?" Cam whispers into the shell of my ear.

"I know I shouldn't care, but I'm a little worried. Why is that guy acting like that?" I don't expect him to tell me, neither of them share anything with me usually, but when he sighs and opens his mouth to speak again, my interest is piqued.

"Warren is unhinged. He's very much like us, a monster that hides beneath a mask. His relationship with his girl is complicated, and if I had to guess, I'm going to assume she disappeared, and he knew nothing about it. So, since she's not here to bear his wrath, he takes it out on everyone and everything in sight."

"Sounds like he needs therapy," I blurt out without thinking.

Cameron snorts, a bubble of laughter escaping his lips, "We all need some type of therapy, but that shit is stupid. Sitting in a room with someone, talking out your problems. Pfft, breaking stuff, and learning to cope with it on your own is easier."

"How do you cope?" I question.

"I have you…" he answers without question.

I open my mouth to respond when the bedroom door opens, and Easton steps inside, closing the door behind him. His eyes are dark, and his face is serious.

"We need to get out of here for a little while. He's going to self-destruct, and I don't think having her here is going to help." Easton speaks as if I'm not sitting right in front of him.

"Okay," Cam says, ungluing himself from my side. As soon as he's gone, I miss the warmth his body gave me. "Let's go do some shopping. She needs some clothes anyway."

Easton's lips turn up into a grin, "Yeah, that would be fun, we can dress up our little doll however we want."

Ignoring the fact that they are talking about me like I'm not here, I insert myself into the conversation. "Did you just say that you are taking me out shopping?" Excitement sparks inside of me. I haven't been out of this house in two days.

"Yes, let's go. Just don't have the stupid idea to try and run away from us."

I almost roll my eyes. "I won't." *Probably not, unless I get a really good chance.* "But... you know I don't have any money, right?"

Easton shrugs, "We'll pay. Plus, we technically owe you payment for your *dancing*."

I haven't danced for them, and knowing what he is talking about makes my stomach churn. I don't want them to pay me for sex.

Cam must be reading my mind because he gives me a soft smile and helps me off the bed. "Don't think about it like that, sweetheart."

I can feel Easton's eyes on me, tracking every step I take like a predator. I won't say it out loud, but it will be nice to have clothes of my own, even though I know that letting them buy them for me will mean I'm indebted to them in another way.

Walking out of the bedroom, Cameron takes the lead holding my hand in his while Easton follows behind us. When they are being nice to me like this, holding my hand, and doing stuff for me, I can almost forget why I'm here. If it could always be this way...

My thoughts evaporate into smoke when I hear glass breaking somewhere in the house. Cameron pauses in the entryway and exchanges a look with Easton. It's so strange because though they aren't brothers, they act as if they are in every way.

"Put your shoes on," Cameron orders me, and I slip my feet into the single pair of sneakers beside the door. Ushering me out of the house and to the car, Cameron releases my hand and slides into the driver's seat while Easton sits beside me in the back.

An electric current ripples between us. We're like fire and gasoline right now, one spark and everything could catch on fire. Doing my best to ignore the blistering heat between us, I place my hands in my lap and look out the window.

"Does this mean my house arrest is over?" I direct my attention to Cameron, but Easton clears his throat and answers.

"No, it's just started. When you prove you can be trusted, then it'll be lifted."

"I have proven I can be trusted. I haven't told anyone about James." I twist in my seat to face him. I'm aware I'm taunting a beast, but I'm tired of him never showing any emotion but anger. I want to know what lurks deeper beneath the surface. I want to see what makes him tick.

"Do you want to end up like James?" Easton taunts.

Even though I know he can't be serious, there is still a sliver of fear that fills my belly.

"You wouldn't kill me." I cross my arms over my chest. In a split second, I'm being dragged across the seat by my hair.

Gasping, I fight against Easton's grasp, a shudder rippling down my spine when his teeth nip at my earlobe, "Give me a reason to test that theory, and I'll prove to you just how bad Cameron and I can be."

"Easton," Cameron warns from the front seat, but he doesn't release me yet.

"We can be the biggest, scariest monsters you've ever seen, or we can be two gentlemen that only treat you and fuck you like a whore behind closed doors. Only you decide what happens."

Without warning, he releases me, and I remain like that, sprawled across his lap. Easton smirks like the devil who was just sold someone's soul.

That snaps me out of it, and I scurry across the seat. I try to ignore the way my core burns, and my insides tingle with anticipation. Is it possible that I'm sick? Mentally ill? Or just Stockholm syndrome? Why did that turn me on? It's wrong, and yet I want him to do it again.

To wrap his hand up in my hair and force his cock into my mouth. Yes, something is very wrong with me.

"Stop taunting him, Stella," Cameron calls, and when I look up, I find him grinning in the rearview mirror at me. He thinks this is funny. Well, it's not. None of this is funny. I press my lips into a firm line and remain quiet the rest of the drive. Just as Cameron is parking, I see that he's brought us to the mall.

Oh, joy.

"Don't try anything funny, or I swear to god, I will take you over my knee and spank your ass before I fuck it so everyone within a two-block radius can hear."

I know his words are supposed to be a fearful warning, but they aren't. It does something entirely different to me. Not that I'm going to tell him that. Together we all get out of the car and walk into the mall. It's strange how normal this feels, especially since it shouldn't feel this way. I don't feel like myself as excitement zings through me as Easton and Cam guide me through each store.

They encourage me to try anything and everything on, and even though I tell them I don't want something, they make sure I get it simply by sliding their card at the checkout like it's no big deal.

While Cameron and Easton are rough, dark, and scary, they've changed my life for the better. It feels like they've taken from me, and they have in many ways, but they've given to me too. After we shop, we share lunch together in the food court, and I even get Easton to smile, which is a very rare occurrence.

On the way out to the car, we pass a group of girls who glare at me and bat their lashes at the guys. I have no reason to feel jealous, but I do. It feels like Easton and Cameron are mine, and having those girls look at them, it enrages me.

I toss my bags into the back of the car and get into the backseat, Easton following behind me. On the way home, I tell myself that regardless of how things have been, my life has never been as good as it is right now. Grams is happy and taken care of, which is something I could never offer her if I was still working in the kitchen at the university.

"Do you think I could go and see Grams again soon?" I ask.

"We can arrange something, yes, but Cam or I will be with you during your visit."

I shrug, "That's fine, but just to warn you, you'll be bored the entire time. Grams is either knitting or watching tv."

Easton grins, "I like visiting with Grams, so I'm not bothered by that at all. Plus, it gives me a chance to make sure that the hospital is keeping up on their end of the bargain."

"Which is what?" I counter, curious as to what he offered the hospital. I knew it was him and Cameron that had something to do with Grams' treatment change, but I can't pinpoint what it is that they would've said? Threatened them, maybe? Offered them money? The possible ways this could go are endless.

"Nothing you have to worry about," Easton dismisses the topic, and I cross my arms, feeling like a child all over again.

"I'll take you to see Grams this week," Cameron announces from the front, saving the day and me from spiraling down a monstrous hole of emotions.

"Thank you," I reply, feeling a little less upset by Easton's dismissal. Though I'm not completely their equal, I'm being given everything I could ever want or need, and that's worth being grateful for because the alternative could be way worse.

20

EASTON

"Ever been drunk, princess?" I ask as we sit in Cameron's bedroom. I just got back from classes, and Cam has been home all day cuddling, and doing god knows what with Stella. If he was anyone else, I'd be slaughtering him, but Cam is like a brother to me, and sharing with him is like breathing. It's natural.

"Stop calling me that," Stella lashes out with annoyance, "I'm not a princess. In fact, I'm far from one."

Damn right.

I grin, seeing her get all worked up, "Okay, have you ever been drunk, *Stella*?" Her name rolls off my tongue thickly, and all I can think about is the things I could do with that tongue between her thighs. God, I have to stop thinking about that, or I'm going to have to fuck her before we leave.

"No," she answers bashfully.

"This should be fun," Cam snorts.

"What should be fun?" she asks, looking between us.

"We're going to take you somewhere. To see if you can hang with the Blackthorn Elite," Cam answers without giving her any other information.

Stella perks up, "Wait, we're going to a party?" Even though she tries to hide it, I can see her excitement.

"We are, and in case you were wondering, yes, this is a test," I narrow my gaze on her face, dropping slowly to her full, pink lips. I have this strange urge to kiss her, to taste her, to draw out her feelings, and see if they mirror my own.

"Of course, it is. What do I wear?" She blinks, breaking eye contact.

Cam smiles widely, "That little red cocktail dress we bought you the other day. Wear that."

Stella's face fills with horror, "No, it's too short, and I already told you both that I would never wear that scrap of fabric out of the house."

Crossing my arms over my chest, I can feel the anger rolling through me. Stella isn't good at taking orders, but I don't give a shit. She needs to learn to do what she's fucking told. This is the precise reason we're at loggerheads right now.

"I don't remember asking you if you wanted to wear it."

Sitting up a little straighter, she flickers her gaze between Cam and me before settling her gaze back on mine.

"Do you really want everyone to see what is yours?"

I almost grin. *Almost.*

"So, we're playing this game now, huh?" I taunt.

Something close to fear sparks in her gray eyes, "Cam," she pleads softly, looking to him for help, but little does she know, Cam isn't running this show. I am.

"He can't help you, and even if he could, he wouldn't." I curl my lip, anger boiling over at the audacity she has to look to him, "You're going to wear the dress, and yes, everyone will look at you, but they will know when they see you with us that you're ours, and that will be significant enough for them, and if it isn't, then we will handle it. But you're wearing that dress, even if I have to put it on you myself."

My jaw aches as I clench it, waiting for her objection, but it never comes. Instead, she gets up and walks into the closet. A second later, she appears before me, the dress in her hands. She strips out of her clothes, and I can't stop myself from dragging my gaze over her naked chest and bare belly.

Full tits that my cock would fit perfectly between.

Fuck. I'm hard as steel in an instant, and I curl my hands into tight fists to stop myself from reaching out to touch her. Maintaining eye contact, she steps into the dress and shimmy's it up her body. I watch her body disappear beneath the tight fabric and damn near curse when she turns around, holding the dress in place with her hands.

"At least zip me up," she says, tossing some of her blonde hair over her shoulder. I want to bite that soft skin, mark her.

Out of the corner of my eye, I can see Cameron snickering on the bed.

Fucker.

"Of course," I force my fist to uncurl and grab onto the tiny zipper, dragging it upward. As soon as she's completely zipped up, I drop my hand and take a step back. She whirls around, and I drink her in, getting my first view of her. The dress hugs her body perfectly, and her breasts swell out the top.

Maybe she was right, she shouldn't wear this thing out of the house. Fuck, if I tell her that though.

"Happy?" She crosses her arms over her chest, drawing my attention back to her breasts. Fuck me.

Swallowing down my arousal, I refuse to let her know how hard I am for her right now, and how right she is about not wearing this dress out of the house.

"Very," I force a smile, knowing damn well I'll be in at least one fistfight by the end of the night.

∼

STELLA STICKS out like a flower in a field full of weeds as she brings the cup to her lips. She doesn't belong here, with us, mingling with the Blackthorn assholes. Not because she's less than people here, but because she is better than us.

She's kind, sweet to the core and naive in the best ways. Anyone in this room can see that from a mile away. All of us are corrupted by money, sex, and secrets. Her, she's like a butterfly, innocent, beautiful, full of light. Free, with nothing holding her back.

Parker and his girlfriend, Willow, show up shortly after we arrive. Annoyingly, Stella becomes glued to Willow's side. They drink and mingle, and even I find myself relaxing a little, sipping at my beer, and watching Stella as she enjoys herself, maybe a little more than she should.

"Shit, that bitch is coming over here," Cameron elbows me in the side, and I drag my gaze away from Stella and over to Carly, who is headed toward us like a heat-seeking missile.

"Easton," she coo's once within earshot, batting her long thick lashes at me like that's going to get me to undo my pants and fuck her.

"Carly," I greet, letting my eyes roam over her. She's wearing a dress similar to Stella's but where Stella is soft, real, and innocent. Carly is fake, not only in the way she acts but in every sense of the word. She hides behind makeup and her daddy's money, and I'm not interested in that. But that doesn't mean I can't pretend to be.

I can feel Stella watching me, and I allow myself to sneak a look at her. Her delicate jaw is clenched, and she looks like a kitten ready to explode with anger.

"Want to go upstairs?" Carly steps closer and places a well-manicured hand against my chest. I look down at it, and then over at Stella. A few weeks ago, I would have said yes in a heartbeat, but now the only person I'm interested in is Stella. I have to admit, I do like seeing her reaction right now. I like seeing the fire in her eyes flicker, it tells me that she's in just as deep with us as we are with her.

Realizing my attention isn't on her, Carly twists around, her gaze pinning Stella.

"Who the hell are you?" Carly sneers, flipping her bleach blonde hair over her shoulder. "I don't remember inviting you."

Stella blinks, slowly, her face a mask of confusion as she looks between Carly and me.

"Stella, and I'm here with Easton and Cameron."

Carly places a hand on her hip, "Oh, are you now?"

"Yes, I am."

"Funny, I've never seen you with them before. Do you go to Blackthorn, or are you a cheap stripper they hired?" Carly purses her lips and bats her eyes. Cam moves to take a step, most likely going to interject, but I give him a look that tells him to let things play out.

"I... I'm..."

Carly taps her foot impatiently. "You're what? A stripper or a whore? Too stupid to get into Blackthorn? Or just too poor? Tell me, please."

My teeth grind together at each insult that Carly slings at her. She's a fucking bitch but telling her that will only inflate her ego.

"Wait," Carly gasps. "I have seen you before. You work in the cafeteria." She tips her head back and starts laughing like someone just told her the funniest joke ever.

"Stop being a bitch, Carly," Willow cuts in before Stella can respond.

"Me? I'm not being a bitch. Just wondering why the help is trying to be one of us." Carly smiles, but she looks more like a shark showing off all her teeth.

Willow rolls her eyes, "I'm sure you've got more important things to do than bully her." Parker, who was talking to some guy off to the side, hears Willow talking and walks up to her side. He takes in the scene before him and pierces Carly with a glare.

Like a dog, Carly cowers, tucking her tail between her legs. That's the thing about Parker. He doesn't hide his darkness; he wears it like a medal of honor, and anyone who fucks with him or his girl will be taken out by it.

"Get lost, Carly," I finally speak up, wanting her to just be gone.

Carly's red-painted lips form into a firm line, and it's obvious she wants to tell me to fuck off, but with Parker standing there, she doesn't have the balls. He runs this school and holds all the power in his hands.

"Whatever, I guess we let anyone into these parties nowadays," she scoffs and walks away like her shit don't stink.

Willow places a gentle hand on Stella's shoulder. "Are you okay?"

"Yeah, I'm fine. I need to go get another drink." She forces herself to smile, probably expecting me to believe it, but she doesn't know how much I watch her, how much I know about her. I know what makes her happy, what her face looks like when she falls apart. I know that even when she says she hates her punishments, she really deep down enjoys them.

Shouldering past us, she gives me a dirty look, one that promises pain, and all I can do is smile. *Show me your worst, baby, and I'll show you mine.*

"Are you going to follow her?" Cam leans over and asks.

Bringing the cup to my lips, I take a sip of the frothy beer.

"Yeah, I want to see what she does first. See if she makes a run for it," I reply, watching the entrance of the kitchen like a hawk. If she runs, then I'll give chase, and like a wolf, I won't stop till I have her in my grasp.

21

STELLA

*T*ears sting my eyes as I walk into the kitchen to make myself another drink. I can feel everyone looking at me like I'm some kind of sideshow. Is that why they brought me here? To look down on me? To make me feel small and unimportant? To remind me that I am less, that I'm not one of them, and that I will never fit in?

Without checking the label, I grab a liquor bottle and pour some amber liquid into my red plastic cup. I take a sip, swallowing the alcohol and letting it burn all the way down my throat before it settles heavy in my stomach. I briefly close my eyes, trying to drown everyone around me out, pretending I'm curled up in my own bed, with Grams knitting down the hall.

"Bad day?" A male voice pierces through the heavy fog. I blink my eyes open and find some guy standing next to me, a beer in his hand, a smile on his face.

For a few seconds, I just stare at him, surprised that someone is approaching me at all, let alone a guy. Glancing over his shoulder, I see Easton glaring at me, but he doesn't make a move to intervene.

I don't know if it's the alcohol or if I'm simply losing my mind, but in this moment, all I want to do is lash out. I want to hurt them like they hurt me by bringing me here. Like they hurt me by not saying anything when Carly belittled me.

Just once, I want to do something to them.

"Terrible day," I finally answer. Remembering how Carly touched Easton, I do the same with the stranger. Running my hand over his chest, I force the words out. "Maybe you can make it a little better?"

His eyes light up, and a triumphant smile spreads across his face. He isn't a bad looking guy, typical jock with perfect hair, and a megawatt smile, but he has nothing on Easton or Cam. The thought angers me further, no matter what, they're inside my head, weaseling their way into every thought. I move a little closer, wanting to push the limits as much as I can.

"I'm sure I could, sweetheart." He cups my cheek, and I cringe at the pet name but manage to keep a straight face. I let my hand drift over his chest and inhale his cologne while trying to hide my disgust of the whole situation when Easton appears out of nowhere.

One moment the guy is standing in front of me, and the next, he is pinned against the closest wall. I can't make sense of the scene before me; everything is moving too fast. When I finally gather my wits, I find Easton has him by the collar with one hand, the other is clenched into a fist ready to punch the guy.

"Easton, we were just talking." I cut in, trying to defuse the situation, knowing damn well that it was more than that.

"I'm sorry, man. I didn't know she was with you. I just walked in." The guy defends himself, holding up his hands as if to say he's innocent, and really, he is. This entire thing is on me.

Easton slowly drops his hand, and a sigh escapes my lips. I start to walk toward him when over his shoulder he grins at me, that signature smile of his tells me all I need to know. A dreadful feeling gathers in my gut a moment before Easton rears back his fist, punching the guy in the stomach.

"Don't ever fucking touch what is mine again," he snarls and releases him with a shove. I watch as the nameless guy doubles over, holding onto his stomach, the drink in his hand falling to the floor, splattering brown liquid everywhere.

"Fuck you! I'm not yours!" I hiss as I scurry from the room, wanting to put as much distance as possible between us.

Looking around, I see an open door in the hallway. I sprint across the hall, through that door which I quickly realize leads to a bathroom. I try to shut the door behind me, but before the lock clicks in, someone pushes the door in and me with it.

I'm about to keep yelling at Easton when I look up and see that it is not him at all. It's Carly.

"Where are you off to so fast?" she asks, pushing me back so hard she almost knocks me on my ass. While she locks the door behind her, I try to gather my wits and compose myself.

"What do you want?" I answer her question with a question.

"Just wanted to clear things up between us," she snaps, folding her arms in front of her chest.

"What's that supposed to mean? There is nothing to clear up."

I hate you. You hate me. The end.

"Listen, I am not the bad guy here. Really, I am doing you a favor by giving it to you straight. You don't belong here, and you definitely do not belong with Easton or Cameron. Everybody knows it, most of all, Easton and Cam. I just mean that you shouldn't fool yourself. You are nothing to them, but a cheap hooker they're gonna have some fun with."

"You don't know what is going on between us." I try to defend myself and my relationship with the guys, but I know I don't have a leg to stand on. I know she is right.

Someone knocks on the door, but both of us ignore the sound.

"You can't honestly believe there is anything going on, other than you getting paid to spread your legs? You are a class-A gold digger and not a good one at that."

"Open the damn door!" Easton yells from the hallway, making me jump.

"Of course, hold on," Carly answers while giving me a vindictive smile that makes me shudder. She turns to open the door. Cam and Easton appear in the doorframe, both looking like they are about to lose their shit. "We're done here anyway."

"Time to go, Stella," Easton growls at me. Cam motions for me to come to him, and my legs move all on their own.

Stepping around Carly, I follow the guys through the house and outside. Neither one of them looks the entire time. When we get to the car, Cam opens the back door for me and ushers me in. Closing the door behind me, I watch as they both get into the front seat.

"What were you fucking thinking? You want me to kill someone else? Or you just want to piss us off?" Easton asks through clenched teeth as we pull away from the frat house.

"Maybe I wanted you to see what it feels like."

"*What it feels like?*" Easton's voice booms through the car. "I didn't fucking throw myself at the next best thing. You did! Looked mighty desperate too if you ask me." I know he is saying those words to hurt me, and he doesn't miss his mark. They leave a terrible sting behind, and the sick feeling in my gut spreads throughout my body.

"You messed up, Stella. You shouldn't have done that," Cameron finally speaks up, disappointment dripping from his words. "We told you this was a test, and you failed miserably."

"Sorry, I don't measure up to your standards," I bark, the alcohol in my veins not helping at all. Crossing my arms, I sink back into the seat like a small child. "I guess I'll try to do better on our next outing."

"Next?" Easton scoffs. "You really think we're gonna take you anywhere after that shitshow? You're lucky if you'll ever leave the bedroom again."

I refuse to look at him. I'm angry with myself, with them, with the entire situation. I hate that I'm acting this way, that I got that guy hurt because of my actions.

"All I wanted was for you to feel the same pain I'm feeling..."

"That's just it, Stella," Easton turns in his seat, and I can feel his eyes on me, but I don't dare glance at him. Instead, I focus on a speck of dust clinging to the window. "In order to hurt my feelings, I'd have to have them, to begin with. So next time you provoke me, remember that."

Forcing myself to look at him, I let my gaze collide with his before I whisper, "I will."

I'm tired of longing for something more when there isn't anything to hope for.

22

CAMERON

For days now, Easton and Stella have been at each other's throats. I try to diffuse the situation, but I can't make either of them happy. Stella needs things from us that I am not sure we can give her. Yes, I have feelings for her, and they're growing every day, but Easton isn't like me. He's more stubborn and much harder to convenience.

The tension in this house is at an all-time high, and for once, it's not the sexual kind. I'm not sure how to deal with it, but the way we have been isn't working.

Stella is curled up on the couch watching some chick flick while Easton is sitting at the table, writing a paper for class, on his laptop. I'm sitting on the recliner, scrolling through my phone, enjoying the quiet and peace. I look up from my phone, and it's almost like I know it won't last long...

The doorbell rings, and I shoot a questionable glance to Easton. He shakes his head, answering my silent question on if he was expecting anyone. *I guess not.*

Setting my phone on the coffee table, I get up and go to open the door. As soon as I do, I wish I had never gotten up.

"Hey, sexy," Chelsey, a girl I *used* to occasionally fuck greets me and pushes past me and into the house without waiting for my invitation.

"Whoa, hold on. I don't have time for this," I tell her, grabbing her by the arm, but she shrugs out of my hold and steps further into the foyer. Now she is close enough to the living room that Stella can see her. *Great.*

"What the hell are you doing here, Chelsey?" I growl, trying to keep my voice low.

"You," she snickers, turning to face me, a giant smile on her face. "Who's the girl sitting on your couch, and why is she dressed?"

"None of your business. Now, get out."

"Why so mean? I just got back into town and wanted a quick fuck. If you're not down, tell Easton I'm available."

"I'm busy," Easton's gruff voice echoes from the dining room.

"Busy with her?" Chelsey points toward Stella, who is looking at us with wide eyes.

"Yes. I'll call you when I'm done with her, okay?" I say simply to get rid of her. "Neither one of us is interested right now, so leave."

"Come on. We can include her..." She frowns, giving me her best pouty face, but none of that works on me.

"Leave," I repeat, firmer this time. She rolls her eyes, but heads toward the door.

"Fine, but call me when you are ready to have your dick sucked properly." She shoots Stella a dirty look and walks to the door.

"Will do," I say without thinking. I just want her out of the house and gone. As soon as she steps outside, I close the door and lock it behind her. I turn the doorbell off on my way back to the living room, just in case, she doesn't get the picture.

No more unwanted visitors.

As soon as I enter the living room, I can feel Stella staring at me. She's looking at me like she wants to accuse me of something.

"Say whatever it is that you want to say," I sigh and make my way over to the couch.

"Who was she?"

"Some girl," I answer.

"That we used to fuck," Easton adds, and I kinda-sorta want to throw my phone at the back of his head.

Stella's body tenses, "So, I'm not the first, and I suppose I won't be the last. No surprise there, I guess."

Wanting to manage the situation before it blows out of proportion, I ask, "What are you talking about?"

"Carly told me that all I'll ever be to you guys is a fuck toy, and as soon as you get bored, you'll be kicking me out. I didn't want to believe it, but every single sign points me further in that direction."

Easton shoves from his chair, causing it to scrape across the floor, "It's not like she's wrong." He walks into the living room, his eyes dark and taunting as he stares down at Stella, who looks pissed.

"Stop pretending like you don't care, stop acting like nothing is going on between us. We might have started out where there was nothing between us, but things have changed."

The air grows thick, and I know once again, shit is about to go down.

"Why don't you stop looking deeper into things? Carly wasn't lying. You're our fuck doll. We don't keep women around because we want a relationship, we keep them as long as they're a good lay. That's all you'll ever be to us. Why can't you get that in that head of yours? We pay you, you spread your legs. That's all."

I can see the exact moment her heart cracks down the middle. Her emotions are written clearly on her face, anger, disbelief, and regret flicker in her eyes, but mostly it's just bone-crushing sadness. I wish I could tell her that he doesn't mean what he just said, but I don't know how to get him to admit more is going on here.

If he feels it, he isn't letting on.

Like I expected, Stella turns her sad gaze to me, and all I can do is look away.

"Tell her, Cam, tell her that's all she'll ever be to us."

I feel as if I'm being tugged in two directions. Part of me wants to tell Stella she means more than that, but part of me knows there isn't any point. I'm not cut out for this, for anything more than what we have right now, and Easton, he's beyond unstable.

Digging deep, I swallow my emotions down and lift my chin, looking her straight in the eyes. She's staring at me, pleading with me to disagree, but I can't.

"That's all you'll ever be," the words roll off my tongue so easily, but I can feel them piercing my heart. I hate myself a little more as her face falls, and her feelings crumble like dry clay in her hands right before my eyes.

"I... I don't believe you. Either of you." Her eyes glisten with unshed tears, and she gets up, trying to escape from us. Without another word, she leaves the room, probably to cry somewhere.

I glare at Easton. *What an asshole. Who am I kidding, I'm not any better!*

With her gone, I sink deep into the couch cushion, wishing it would swallow me whole.

"You know we can't develop feelings for her, right?" Easton asks, running a hand through his hair. He looks haunted, and tired, so fucking tired. I stare at him for a long second before I tell him what I've been wanting to tell him for a while now.

"I'm past developing feelings. I'm already there. I want her, need her, but I don't know how to make this work. This whole situation is so screwed up."

Easton appears shocked, his mouth popping open and then snapping closed a moment later. "I... I don't know how to handle that."

"You don't have to handle it. They are my feelings."

"Whatever," he shakes his head. "She's nothing, just a girl who saw us do some bad shit." He gives me his back and walks into the kitchen. "We did this to keep her quiet. That's all it will ever be."

"Keep telling yourself that," I mumble under my breath, hoping and praying that he can come out on the other side and see this for what it is.

This might've started as revenge, as a way to keep her mouth shut, but it's turned into way more than I could've ever imagined. Stella is past being the girl we need to keep quiet. She's now the one and only person to ever get inside our hearts.

23

STELLA

When you put something under too much pressure, it snaps, and I guess that's what happened to me. Something inside my mind snapped and cracked straight down the middle.

"You know what we'll do if you try to leave, right?" Cameron's voice cuts through my mind, interrupting my thought process.

"What?" I question, trying to act like I wasn't ignoring him.

"Don't do anything stupid while we're gone. We're going to lock you in here, and you are going to stay here. Be a good girl, and we'll give you more freedom again."

I nod, my throat throbbing as emotions I can't fully explain ripple through me. I'm falling for these men, falling helplessly for them, but they don't see me the same way. They just see me as the girl who caught them killing someone. The girl they own and can do whatever they want with.

That's why I need to leave, I need to get away from them. In the last few days, I've been on my best behavior, playing the role of the good little prisoner, waiting for a chance just like this. I was hoping they would leave me alone, and now that they are doing it, I'm going to use that time to make a run for it.

I just wish this wasn't so hard. I wish they meant nothing to me. I should hate them, but instead, I'm falling deeper every day. Maybe I'm wrong about all of this, maybe I just have Stockholm syndrome. Let's be real, I don't know what love is. This all might be a fucked up mind game to them, and I just think I love them.

Either way, they clearly don't feel the same for me, and I refuse to stick around and be made a fool off. I won't wait for them to take the hint. I'll take Grams and go somewhere else. I'll figure it out.

"When will you be back?" I push off the mattress. Easton stands in the doorway staring at me. His mood swings are giving me whiplash. One moment he looks at me like I'm the most important thing in the world, the next, he glares at me like he wants to kill me. The only time I feel as if I'm truly connected to him is when we have sex, and I can't take it anymore. I want, *no*... I need more from him.

"Doesn't matter, all that matters is that you stay in this room. Don't give us another reason to punish you." I stop myself from rolling my eyes at Cam.

"Of course, you seemed to enjoy the last punishment, so I wouldn't be all that surprised if you disobeyed just for the fun of it," Easton chimes in.

This time I do roll my eyes, "I'll be here when you get back." The lie rolls off my tongue so easily, I worry they might not believe me with how fast I reply.

"Better be, because next time we won't take it so easy on you," Cam whispers as he leans in to press a kiss to my forehead.

"Got it. I'll be here," I tell them both and pretend to be interested in the stack of paperbacks that they bought me, that rest on the nightstand.

Cam moves toward the door, gripping the handle in his hands. I catch Easton's dark gaze glittering with excitement, almost as if he's waiting for me to screw up just so he has a reason to punish me. He's fucked up. Actually, all of this is fucked up because while he wears his arousal and excitement on the outside, my own bubbles just beneath the surface.

It's hard for me to admit that I liked what they did to me, that I didn't just like it but that I've wanted it to happen again since that night.

"Be good," Cam says, closing the door. The door clicks shut, and then the lock is engaged. I wait, listening as their footsteps recede away from the bedroom. I wait for about ten more minutes after I hear the car leave to make certain that they are actually gone. Then I get out my phone and call Katie.

"Hello?" She answers on the third ring.

"Hey, Katie… it's Stella." I stutter, trying to remain calm. I can't believe I'm going to do this, but then again, what other options do I have? I need to think for myself and decide if this is really what I want. I need to see if my absence will change anything.

"Hey, girl, what's up? You doing okay?"

"No, actually, I could really use your help."

"What is it?"

"Could you come pick me up from Cam and Easton's house?"

"Yes, of course. When? Now?"

"Ah… yes, can you? If it's not too much trouble?"

"No, boo, don't be ridiculous. I'll be right there." She hangs up before I can give her directions, and for a moment, I'm not sure if I should call her back. Then I wonder if she knows where they live already, it's then, I remember that they know each other from the strip club.

Shit, maybe they used to date? Could that be why the guys got so mad at me for meeting up with her? I didn't even think of that, maybe they didn't want us hanging out, maybe they were worried she would tell me something about them? As if knowing they murdered someone, didn't deter me enough.

I grab the chair from the far corner of the room and pull it across the floor, stopping once I reach the window. Opening it slowly, I press against the wire screen. My fingers shake as I push on the two bottom corners, yet it doesn't take much effort to get the screen popped out. I tug it out of the frame and release it, watching as it falls to the ground.

It's not a far drop, and thankfully so, because I'm not about to break my bones getting out of here. I swing my leg over the ledge and let my body hang out, lowering myself slowly until I'm hanging from the windowsill by my fingertips.

Sucking in a deep breath, I let myself fall. Even with me bending my knees when my feet touch the ground, there is a sharp pain that shoots through my legs, and I groan as I land on my ass with a thud. *Ugh, that hurt.*

Getting up, I rub my hands over the front of my jeans to wipe the dirt off of them before I walk toward the road. I'm almost to the side street when my phone starts to ring. I pull it out and look at the screen, seeing Katie's name flash across it.

Answering it, I try not to sound as winded as I feel, "Hey."

"I'm parked one street over; do you want me to drive to the house?"

"No, I... I'll walk." I force air into my lungs, "I'll see you in a second or two." I end the call and shove the phone back into my pants pocket. My gaze sweeps up and down the street, paranoia trickling into my mind. My heart thunders in my chest as I start walking, each step feels like it takes an eternity. As I appear on the street, Katie rolls up in a white car. She stops directly in front of me and waves for me to get in. For one single second, I consider turning around and going back to the house. Call it a sixth sense or gut feeling, but it feels wrong to be getting into this car.

Knowing that if I don't leave now, I never will, I grab the door handle and pull the door open. Hunkering down in the seat, I close the door behind me, and Katie hits the gas, and we zoom off down the street.

"Where do you want to go?" She questions as she turns out of the subdivision.

"I don't know. I don't have anywhere to go." I hadn't thought this far ahead. I don't have a place for Grams yet, so she has to stay where she is for now. I know Cam and Easton won't go after her. They might be crazy, but they don't hurt little old ladies.

Katie taps on her chin with her finger, her lips pursed, and her eyes narrowed as if she's thinking. "Oh, I know a place you could stay for a while. Don't worry, girl. I've got you."

Glee fills my veins. "Thanks, seriously... thank you. You have no reason to help me, yet you always do."

"Yup, that's me. Here to help," Katie smiles as we drive further out of town. My stomach rolls with nervous energy.

"Where are we going?"

"My place," she answers without looking away from the road.

"You don't live in the city?"

"No, not quite. Just a little bit out. We'll be there shortly."

"Okay," I nod, looking out of the window as houses and trees whoosh by me. A short while later, I realize that there are almost no houses on the road anymore. Only a few houses scattered here and there but all far apart from each other. I wonder how far she lives out.

"You must have like no neighbors," I try to joke, breaking the awkward silence.

"Yeah, not really. You know being with a bunch of people at work, I enjoy my peace and quiet when I'm home. Plus, a house outside the city was much cheaper. I was able to get a bigger, newer house for half of the money."

"That makes sense."

"You know if you decided to work at Night Shift, you could afford a house on your own too." I swallow thickly, it feels like the weight of the world is resting on my shoulders. Get a job, find a place to live, take care of Grams, and figure out what the hell is going on inside my head.

"I just don't know if I can. Plus, Cam and Easton would find me there in a heartbeat."

"What's up with you and them anyway? I've never seen them take a girl home. I mean other than for... you know? A quick fuck."

Jealousy burns hot in my veins at her mentioning *my* guys sleeping with other girls. *My guys?* No, that's wrong, they will never be mine, just as I will never be theirs.

"That's all I am to them." I frown out the window.

"I doubt that. I've seen the way they look at you." She presses on the breaks, and the car slows before she turns into the driveway leading up to an older looking farmhouse. The yard is unkempt, and the porch is filled with clutter, which gives the place a creepy feel.

"This is it, home sweet home," Katie says, cutting the engine. She gets out of the car, and I follow her to the porch. Wrapping my arms around myself, I wait as she unlocks the front door.

The same uneasy feeling I felt when I got into her car creeps up on me again, and for a moment, I think about running the other way and calling Easton and Cam.

"I'm starving!" Katie interrupts my thoughts. "Have you eaten yet? I have some leftover pasta in the fridge, do you want some?"

"Ah, sure..." I've eaten already, but I couldn't bring myself to eat a lot for lunch. My mind was too busy thinking about my escape. Katie pushes the front door open and I follow her inside. The moment I step foot in the house, the bad feeling I've been having overwhelms me.

I scan the inside, realizing that it's even dirtier and more cluttered than the outside. Old pizza cartons and crushed up beer cans are scattered around the living room. Dirty clothes and trash are on the floor, and the whole place smells of dust and dirt. But what is most unnerving is the pictures on the wall, they're of a family... a family that doesn't look anything like Katie.

"This isn't your house..."

"No, it's not," Katie confirms, her voice clipped, and all the blood drains from my face. I try to step away from her, turning back toward the door when I hear someone moving behind me. I twist around, but before I can see who it is, a sharp pain erupts at the back of my head.

My knees buckle, and the last thing I think about before hitting the floor is how I should have stayed with Easton and Cameron.

∽

WHEN I COME TO, my head is throbbing, and for a brief second, I think I'm dreaming. Then I realize the ground beneath my body is hard, cold, and that this isn't a dream at all. No, this is a true living nightmare.

"Welcome back," a familiar male voice calls out to me. I look up, and the blood in my veins turns to ice. *Paul.*

I try to get up from the floor just to realize that I am tied up, my arms are numb from being pulled behind my back so tightly. Paul starts laughing as he walks toward me. His face is still black and blue in some spots from where the guys beat him up for touching me. Apparently, he hasn't learned his lesson.

Fear... real fear floods my body. It's a feeling, unlike anything I've ever felt before. Even when Cameron and Easton threatened me, I never felt this kind of terror.

Maybe part of me always knew that they wouldn't hurt me, but Paul, he definitely will. He will tear me apart if he gets the chance, and unfortunately for me, he does now. Helplessly, I wiggle around on the floor, trying to get away from him, but he is on me the next moment.

His meaty fingers digging into my arms as he pulls me up to my feet. I cry out in pain as he pushes me onto the nearby bed, and my head bounces against the headboard.

"Hey, this wasn't part of the plan!" Katie's voice booms through the room, and I pry my eyes open to find her standing in the doorway.

She doesn't look at me, but the expression on her face tells me that she feels ashamed, maybe even sorry.

"I told you, I want my revenge," Paul growls. "Her boyfriends got me fired. This is how I get back at them. I'm gonna fuck their little toy and send it back to them broken."

"Look, I didn't sign up for this part. All I want to know is what happened to my boyfriend?" *Her boyfriend?* "She lives with them. She has to know what they did to James. She has to know something."

Even in my fear clouded mind, I am able to put all the pieces together and see the bigger picture. James was Katie's boyfriend. She must have found out that the guys had something to do with his disappearance. *But how does Paul add into this?*

"Well, how about this. You ask her whatever you want to know, and if she is being a good bitch and tells you everything, then I won't hurt her," Paul grins, and I already know he is full of shit. He will hurt me either way.

"Just tell us, Stella, what did Easton and Cameron do to James?" Katie asks me, pinning me with a gaze that's both desperate and apologetic.

"I-I don't know..." As soon as the words leave my lips, Paul pulls back his hand and swings at me. The palm of his hand makes contact with my face, making my head snap to the side, right before a searing pain erupts across my cheek. The coppery taste of blood fills my mouth, and a whimper escapes my quivering lips.

"Stella," Katie's voice cuts through the fog of pain. "Tell me, and this will all be over. We'll let you go. I promise. I just want to know the truth. I want to know what happened to him."

I wish I could believe her, but even if she was telling the truth, could I tell them? I already know the answer. *No... I couldn't.* I gave Cam and Easton my word, but more than that, I couldn't bear them going to prison, because that would mean I couldn't be with them.

I'm so stupid for having that epiphany now, in the worst time and place. Why couldn't I have realized how much they really mean to me a few hours earlier. I wouldn't be in this mess. I would be safe and sound in bed, waiting for them to return. I should have stayed, should have fought for them instead of giving up so easily.

Swallowing hard, I say quietly, "I'm sorry, Katie. I just don't know..."

"You're a fucking lying bitch!" she yells, hurt dripping like venom from her voice. "Maybe I should leave you two alone for a few hours and see if you remember something then."

"Katie, please," I beg. "You know what he'll do to me."

"Maybe that's what you need. Maybe that's what's going to get you off your high and mighty horse. Too good to work at the strip club? You think I didn't see how you looked at all of us girls working there?"

"Katie, that's not true. I just couldn't do it. I don't think I'm better than anyone," I plead with her, but it falls on deaf ears.

"Lies! You lie! All you do is lie..." She keeps repeating it like she is trying to convince herself. I shake my head, tears falling from the corners of my eyes. "Just do whatever you want to do with her," Katie says, her voice cracking at the end, giving her emotions away. She might not be okay with this, but she turns around and walks out of the room anyway.

Through my tears, I look at Paul, who is smiling like he just won the lottery. "Now, it's time for us to have some fun. Don't you think, Stella?"

Part of me wants to beg, scream, and cry, but I know damn well it won't do me any good. There weren't any houses close by, and Katie is not going to help me. Squeezing my eyes shut, I will my mind to go somewhere else because if I don't, I don't know if I'll survive this.

24

EASTON

I knew it, I fucking knew it. "I told you she would leave! We shouldn't have trusted her. It was a fucking mistake, and I told you so!" I yell as I look out the open window of my room.

"Calm down. This is exactly why we uploaded the tracking app to her phone. Plus, she has no money, she can't have gone far. Pull up the app and find her." Cam tries to calm me while trying to stay calm himself, but I know him well enough to see that he is struggling.

Getting my phone out, I open the app he is talking about, so I can ping her phone. It only takes a few seconds before the red dot appears on the map, but it might as well have been hours. Every moment I don't know where she is and that she is safe feels like a fucking eternity.

"Where is she?" Cam asks impatiently. I tilt the phone in his direction so he can see the screen as well.

"I have no clue where that is? But it's only a twenty-five-minute drive."

"Let's go," Cam says, but we are both already moving. We are out the door and in my car moments later. Cam puts the address into the GPS while I pull out of the driveway and into the road.

The closer we get to the address, the faster my heart is beating, because I don't know what I'm going to do when I get my hands on her. I'm so fucking mad, so mad that I'm worried about actually hurting her this time.

"Where the hell is she?" Cam asks, breaking the silence in the car. I shrug, taking in our surroundings, which is nothing, but trees and a few houses scattered along the road here and there. "We'll be there in five minutes."

Even though I'm already going over the speed limit, I push down the gas pedal a little further. My chest aches now, all these emotions I don't understand swirling around me. I try to concentrate on the most prominent one… anger, but it's hard when there are a plethora of others looming right beneath the surface. Feelings I definitely don't want to deal with.

"This is it," Cam points at a driveway coming up, and I start to slow down. An old farmhouse comes into view, and immediately, a bad feeling settles in my stomach. It's a rundown place that looks like a place someone either sells drugs out of or runs a brothel, or both.

"Looks like shit," I point out the obvious as I drive down the bumpy driveway up to the piece of shit house. There is a car parked in front of the house. When we get closer, I can read the pink glittery bumper sticker clinging to the window, Night Shift.

"That's an understatement. Who the fuck lives here, and why the hell is Stella here?"

"We're about to find out, but according to that bumper sticker someone working at the strip club," I tell him as I put the car in park and cut the engine.

We get out and speed walk across the front yard, and when we walk up to the porch, I catch movement inside the house. When I get closer to the window, I realize it is Katie who is pacing the room.

"Fucking Katie," Cam hisses beside me.

Gritting my teeth, I waltz up to the front door, grab the brass knob and turn it. Of course, it's fucking locked.

"Open the fucking door, Katie, or we'll burn this house to the ground!" I bang my fist against the cracked wood so hard the whole door vibrates. A moment later, the door flies open, and Katie appears looking distraught and scared. Good, she should be afraid.

"I didn't know!" She cries out before I can say a word. "I didn't know he was going to hurt her..."

In a blink of an eye, my rage is flipped upside down and morphs into something entirely different... fear. It's been a long time since I was scared, so long I don't even remember when it was. All I know is that right now, this fear is so strong I feel like it's about to swallow me whole. I don't fear for myself, I'm scared for Stella, scared she is hurt, scared something happened to her, and we couldn't protect her.

The thought of losing her has been swirling around in my head, leaving me on edge for days, but this is different. Losing her because she left us hurts, but losing her because someone took her from us is an almost unbearable thought.

"Who," I growl, "who hurt her?" Katie starts shaking her head, tears falling down the side of her face, but I don't feel the slightest amount of compassion for her. I want to wrap my hands around her neck and force her to tell me who the fuck put their hands on my girl.

"Where is she?" Cam cuts in, his voice frantic.

"Upstairs," Katie whimpers as I push her out of the way and head for the stairs with Cam following close behind. As soon as we make it to the second floor, I hear it, a muffled scream coming from one of the bedrooms.

I've never moved so fast in my life. Not wanting to waste time to see if the door is unlocked, I decide to break it open. Using my body weight, I ram into the door shoulder first. The old wood giving away easily. A loud crack fills the air as the whole lock breaks out of the door frame.

Cam and I burst into the room, and we take in the scene before us. Time seems to slow down as I realize what we are seeing. A fucking horror movie.

I thought I was angry before, but nothing could have prepared me for the all-consuming fury inside of me now. I can feel every muscle in my body vibrating with pure rage.

Stella is on the bed, her hands and feet tied together, and her mouth taped shut. Half of her clothes are ripped off, and her chest is exposed. She is crying, frantically trying to get away from Paul, who is on top of her, straddling her slender body.

I've considered myself a violent person before, but the sick and twisted things running through my mind right now are a new level of fucked up. I want to hurt him, cut him, watch him bleed, and suffer. I want to skin him alive, hear him scream and beg for me to stop. I want to make him suffer beyond measure for putting his filthy hands on Stella.

It takes Paul a moment to realize what's happening, but by the time he jumps up, Cam and I are already on him. With clenched fists, we start beating the living hell out of him. He staggers back, but Cam has a hold on his neck, yanking his face toward us so we can punch him over and over again until his face is bloodied and swollen.

A pained whimper draws me out of my haze, pulling me back to reality like a slingshot. My fist stops mid-air, and I look over my shoulder at Stella.

"Get her, I'll take care of him," Cam tells me, and before I can tell him he should be the one to stay, he is already dragging Paul out of the room.

Turning my attention back to Stella, I rush over to the bed. Now that I get a good look at her face, I can see that it's swollen and red on one side, and her lip is split on the bottom, a small amount of blood trickling down her chin. Another wave of never-ending anger washes over me, but I rein it in, knowing that she needs me right now.

She is looking at me with an expression that has my chest aching. Her eyes hold an ocean of emotions, and I don't know how I can hold my own at bay. Her whole body is shaking, and all I want to do is wrap her into my arms, tell her everything is going to be okay, and that I'll never let her go again.

Before I can do that, I need to get this shit off of her and get her away from this place. I pinch the edge of the tape covering her mouth and pull it off carefully. As soon as she can, she starts talking.

"I-I'm sorry... I'm so sorry. Don't hate me, please," she says in between sobs. "I shouldn't have left—"

"No one hates you," I interrupt her rambling, undoing her restraints at the same time. "Don't worry about anything right now."

The moment she is free, she crawls onto my lap, buries her face into the crook of my neck, and her arms wrap around me so tightly, I don't know if I could pry them off if I wanted to.

"Please don't hate me," she mutters against my skin.

"Stop saying that. No one hates you. I could never hate you. I..." The word is on the tip of my tongue, but I can't bring myself to say it, even though I know it's true. *I love her.*

For a long moment, I just hold her, wondering where Cam took Paul. The house is quiet now and I decide to take her out of here. Wrapping her up in the blanket from the bed, I cradle her against my chest and get up from the bed.

Gently, I carry her through the now empty house. When we get to the car, I realize that the other car is gone now, which means that Katie must have left. I somehow manage to open the door without putting her down. Placing her in the backseat, I'm still burning with rage. I really want to go and find him so I can inflict pain like I want to, but looking at Stella, I know I can't leave her alone. She needs me right now, and knowing that she does is almost as satisfying as going after Paul.

Crawling into the car with her, I pull her shaking body onto my lap and wrap my arms around her. All my anger toward her dissipated when I saw her lying on that bed, completely helpless and mirroring defeat. Instantly, I knew I couldn't deny my feelings for her any longer.

I can't pretend that I don't love her, because all along I knew things had changed between us. She's no longer a person for us to keep quiet. She's the person we share our hearts with.

"I'm-I'm sorry..." She cries, big, fat tears fall from her eyes and slip down her cheeks. "I'm so sorry, I'll be better. I promise." She's remorseful and ashamed, but the only person that should be sorry is Cam and I. Sorry that we pushed her to want to leave. Part of this is our fault, and I'm man enough to admit that.

She never gave us a reason to believe that she was lying, but we kept treating her like she did. We treated her like she was nothing more than our plaything, like she was a fucking prisoner in our home and all because we were too scared of losing her, of telling her how we really feel.

"You don't have to be sorry. I'm sorry, and you definitely don't have to be better. You are already perfect. We'll be better. We should have been better all along." My body is vibrating with anger for myself, for the situation we put her in. I want to break Paul's fingers, one by one.

He touched her, broke her... and he deserves to die for that. As I'm thinking of all the way I want to hurt him, she's shaking in my arms.

"It's okay, baby," I assure her. "Everything is going to be okay..." I trail off, forcing myself to sound calm when really, I'm ready to explode.

The driver's side door opens, and Cam slips into the car. His fists are bloody, and when he looks at me over his shoulder, I can see the disconnect in his eyes.

Did he kill him? I would've.

"He's still alive, but you don't have to worry about him. He is going to jail for a really long time. Our parents are taking care of him. We got to go, they are already on the way here, and we don't want to be here when they arrive."

"What about Katie?" I ask.

There is a darkness in Cam's eyes, and I know he said or did something to ensure that she doesn't open her mouth, I just kind of wish it was me that got to deliver that message to her.

"She won't open her mouth, not unless she wants to spend the rest of her days in prison. I can have James' death pinned on her in a second flat."

"Good, she stepped out of line once, and that got Stella hurt..." My jaw aches as I clench it.

"Relax, no one is going to hurt her ever again," Cam reassures me. I look down at Stella, who has her eyes squeezed shut. Gently, I stroke her face, willing her to open her eyes. I need to see her, feel connected to her; otherwise, I'll get out of this car and murder Paul for touching her.

"Stella, baby, I need you to look at me. I need to see your eyes, because right now I really want to go kill that fucker for touching you, for hurting you." The irony of my words is not lost on me. I hurt her too, we hurt her.

In a flash, her eyes flutter open, and she grips onto my shirt so tightly her knuckles turn white. Her lips wobble as she speaks, "Please, please don't. I-I...need you."

"I love you," I reply, shocking the hell out of both of us.

Cam must not have heard me because he doesn't say anything and instead starts the car. Stella stares up at me with awe in her eyes, and I wish I had told her sooner. Wish I had let myself feel these emotions weeks ago because then maybe this wouldn't have happened.

Stella is quiet the entire way back to the house, but she doesn't let her gaze fall from my own. She stares at me, almost like she doesn't believe what I've told her.

As soon as we arrive at the house, I carry her inside and start to strip off her dirty clothing, looking her over for any injuries. She has a few bruises along her throat and what looks to be a bruise forming on her cheek, but aside from that, she doesn't seem to be injured at all.

"Did he…" I can't even finish the thought. If he touched her there, I will get back in the car, go find him, and kill him. There won't be anything to stop me from doing it either. Damn the consequences, nothing but Stella matters.

Stella sucks her bottom lip into her mouth and gently shakes her head. I sigh outwardly, feeling as if a weight has been lifted off my shoulders.

"Hey, let me give her a shower, and then we can talk afterward about what happens going forward." Cam places a hand on my shoulder, grounding me, and I know I need to get my wicked thoughts together. I knew I was obsessive over her, but I didn't think it could ever feel like this. My heart thunders inside my chest, and I nod my head before running my fingers through my hair.

Breathe. I keep telling myself, but all I want to do is murder Paul. Ruin him, but instead, I force myself to sit on the edge of the bed and watch as Cam takes Stella into the bathroom.

The sound of the shower turning on fills my ears, but I'm still stuck inside my head. We can't continue down this road. We can't let her think she's no one to us, that we're just using her body. It's time to become all or nothing.

When Stella comes walking out of the bathroom, a white towel wrapped around her, all I can do is stare in awe. She is ours, and we're hers, and no matter what happened today, there isn't any way I'm letting her walk out that door. Breaking from the trance, I turn and head to the dresser. I pull out a gray T-shirt and a pair of boxers and turn around and extend them out to her.

Her big gray eyes dart from them and up to my face.

"I'll be right back. I'm going to get dressed, you go help her, and then we can talk." Cam announces as he walks out of the room, a towel slung around his waist.

I nod but don't look away from Stella.

"I'm sorry, I let you down. I'm sorry, I left. I was just… I'm tired of living in the past, Easton. I know I shouldn't want you guys, but I do. I want both of you. I'm falling…" She shakes her head, and strands of wet hair stick to her face. "I'm pretty sure I'm past falling. I love you both, and I don't know how to go forward. I don't know what will happen next."

The pain in her voice, the fear in her eyes, it makes me weak in the knees.

"What happens next is whatever you want."

"Whatever I want?" Her brows furrow in confusion. She doesn't understand, and I get why. She's not used to us letting her have a say, an opinion, or choice. But that changes now.

Cam walks back into the bedroom, fully dressed this time. His eyes dart between us, a question lingering there.

"What do you want, Stella?" Cam asks gently, and I've never been more glad to have him in my life than I am now. We might not be brothers by blood, but we're in every sense of the word. Stella looks between us, her expression completely unreadable.

My heart thuds loudly in my chest. What do I do if she says she wants us to let her go? Looking at her, I don't know how she could love us after all we've done.

"I want to be happy and free. I want you to trust me, to let me leave and go where I want, knowing that I'll always come back to you."

"So, you want to stay?" Cam asks, his voice tight.

Stella nibbles on her bottom lip with indecision, "I do, but only if I can be your equal. It will hurt to leave, but it hurts me more to know that all you see in me is a threat or someone that is less than you. Your secrets are my own now. I would never tell, and I didn't, even when Katie and Paul tried to get me to talk."

Guilt, sadness, and anger gnaw at my insides like a ravenous monster. I should've believed her when she said she wouldn't tell the first million and one times, but I was so caught up in the need to ensure she stayed quiet, I didn't care if I hurt her. I only cared about protecting Cam and me. This is going to change now, there will be one more person in our circle to protect.

Reaching out for her, needing to feel her body beneath my hands, I grab onto her shoulders and pull her into my body. The top of her head reaches the middle of my chest, and I look down at her, wishing I could save her from all the darkness in the world, save her from me.

"I can't go back and change things, and I wouldn't even if I could. What happened lead us to you, and I'll never be able to regret that. I'm not a good person though, and I'm not even sure I could be kind but... I will never make you feel as if you're unequal to us. I will never test your loyalty again. I'm sorry it took me until now to admit that, but I can't let you go. I can't."

"Then don't," she whispers, and I don't stop myself from kissing her then. I let my fingers weave through her damp hair and clamp onto the back of her neck as I kiss her deeper, letting the hunger deep in my veins fill her.

Cam causes the kiss to break sooner than I want, and I let a small growl escape, which he chuckles not so quietly about.

"We're sharing her, asshole," he grins and pulls her into his own arms, forcing me to release her. If I didn't care about him so much, I would punch him in the face and run away with Stella, but there is no me without Cam. We're a brotherhood of our own, and I could never break that kind of bond, not even if I tried.

"Will you both lay down with me?" Stella whispers, a smile tugging at her lips.

"Anything," I answer wholeheartedly. After everything that has happened, I know I'll need to prove myself to her, and I will every day from here on out.

"We'll make this right, Stella. You're more than our equal, you're better than us, you're the queen in our fucked up world." Cam says as he starts to strip out of his clothing. I follow quickly behind, knowing he's never said anything more true before.

She isn't the pawn or bishop anymore. She's the queen in our fucked up kingdom, and we're the kings that were made to protect, cherish, and own her.

All three of us crawl into bed, Stella in the middle. Cam pulls her back to his front, molding their bodies together. I scoot closer, feeling so completely drawn to her, nothing could stop me from taking her into my arms right now. Reaching for me, she lays her hand on my chest, the touch so innocent, so normal, but so life-altering at the same time. I hold her close to my chest and press my lips to her temple. A soft sigh expels from her lips, and a calmness washes over me.

For the first time in months, it feels like all the demons and darkness inside of me have quieted. I place my hand over hers and close my eyes, the steady beat of our hearts mirror together. This is how we belong, the three of us together... always.

EPILOGUE

Stella

"You have your book, folder, calculator, and pencil?" Cameron asks for the third time.

"Yes, I already told you," I smile back at him, tapping my bag.

"I know, but I want to make sure. Professor Barkley is a pain in the ass. It's one of the hardest classes. You sure you want to start with that one? I can still get you out of it."

"I like math, and numbers always came easy to me. I got this, Cam."

"Leave the girl alone, Cam. She is smarter than both of us, and you know it," Easton chimes in, throwing his arm around my shoulders. He kisses my forehead before continuing, "Don't worry, you'll do great, babe."

It's been a few months since the whole Paul thing happened, and my life has changed drastically since then. For the first time since my parents died, I am looking forward to my future, and I'm completely and utterly happy. Which is something I thought I would never be able to say again.

"Go, or you're gonna be late," Easton lets go of me and gives me a gentle shove toward the door. "We'll meet you at the coffee shop by the library after, okay?"

"Okay," I smile, waving at both of them before heading into my very first class at Blackthorn. As soon as I had mentioned my desire to go to college, the guys signed me up for classes. I told them I couldn't afford it, of course, like always, money wasn't an issue to them. I didn't see one bill for my classes. Cam and Easton took care of everything. All I had to do was pick the classes I wanted to take and bam.

Walking into the classroom, I get a few dirty looks, but I'm used to it by now. Some people still think that I don't belong here. Every time Easton and Cameron take me out, there are people staring, but I've gotten to the point where I genuinely don't care anymore.

I can handle the looks, especially since I know no one is going to say anything to my face. Not with knowing who I'm with.

The class goes by fast, and I thoroughly enjoy it. I absorb all the information like a dry sponge. Unlike the guys told me, I don't think this was hard at all. When I walk out, Professor Barkley compliments me on the work I did in class today. I tried my best to interact in the discussions. Excited and downright giddy, I make my way out of the building and head to the coffee shop on the edge of campus. I can't wait to share how the first class went with them.

I turn the corner to the side alley, and my mood turns from great to, oh, my god, what did I just walk into. No way, can I be seeing this right. Looking straight ahead, I see a girl that's being cornered by some guy twice her size. His hands are wrapped around her throat, and he is yelling right into her face. It's like I'm watching a replay of the night Easton and Cameron took me.

"It's your fault. All your fault, and now you dare come here... to

Blackthorn?" He shoves her against the brick, her head bouncing off the hard wall, and all I can do is stand there and watch in horror.

"I didn't know…" She whimpers her entire body shaking. I want to tell her to fight, to stick up for herself, but my mouth won't work.

"Shut up," the guy growls, the deepness of his voice shatters the protective bubble around me, and I force myself out of the trance-like state I'm in. I know that I can't just stand here and watch this happen. I have to do something.

"Stop!" I scream, finally finding my voice.

Drawing all the attention to me is good, but also scary as hell. Both of them look over at me, shock on the man's face, and fear on the girl's and for a split second, I think about just running off to get help instead of putting myself in danger, but that would be a cowardly thing to do, and I'm stronger than that.

Before I can get my legs to move an inch, the guy's gaze narrows, and he releases the girl, taking a step back. I stare at him, taking in his dark features. He's handsome in an I'm-a-dickhead kind of way. Our eyes remain locked as he takes another step backward, and then another before he turns and walks off like nothing happened at all.

What the hell?

"Are you okay?" I rush to the girl's side, taking her hand into my own once he disappears out of the mouth of the alleyway. She is shaking, her face is pale, and a single tear slips down her cheek.

"Yes," she whispers, her big cornflower blues piercing my own. She only lets me hold her hand for a moment before she pulls it out of my grasp. She takes a step back as if she is trying to get away. I don't think she is scared of me, but I get the sense that she doesn't like to be touched. In an instant, I'm even more alarmed. *What happened to this girl?*

"Who was that guy?" I ask, even though it's not really any of my business.

"A friend." She says, brushing a few stray strands of blonde hair from her face.

"He didn't look very friendly to me. In fact, he looked like a grade-A asshole."

Instead of answering she pulls further away, retreating inside of herself. "I-I.. I need to go... thanks again."

"Wait, don't go. We could go somewhere and hang out, do something. My name is Stella," I introduce myself and try to reach for her, but she shakes her head and turns away from me. I watch her speed walk down the alley and disappear behind the corner, wishing I could have done more.

BONUS EPILOGUE

One year later
Cameron

Glancing over at Easton nervously, I listen as the front door creaks open. A second later, it slams closed. I'm giddy with both excitement and fear. I'm pretty sure she'll say yes, but a part of me worries that she'll say no. The last year has been beyond great, but it's been quite a ride for our emotions, and I wouldn't blame her if she ever felt the need to walk out on us. She handles Easton's emotional outbursts like a pro and is there for me whenever I need her.

Figuratively, she is the backbone of our entire relationship.

"Easton, Cam? Where the hell are you guys hiding?" Stella grumbles a moment later, her footsteps coming closer. With each step she takes closer to us, my stomach twists, a boulder of anxiety forming in my gut. The bedroom door is pushed open a second later, and she takes a step forward before realizing we're inside.

As soon as her eyes land on us, her mouth pops open, and her pretty eyes widen with shock. She blinks, taking in the rose petals and candles that litter the room.

"What is this? What's going on?" she croaks.

For a moment, we just stand there, all looking at each other, the words I was going to say stuck in my throat, so I elbow Easton slightly, urging him to talk instead.

"Stella, for the last year, you've been our rock. Really, our everything. You pushed us to be so much more than we ever thought we could be. It took us almost losing you to see what we had was real, but you never gave up," Easton says, giving her his usual devilish grin.

Things aren't always easy between them, but then they have these tender moments when they look at each other, and everything seems to fade away. Or they just fuck the anger out of each other until there isn't anything left.

"You are our queen, and we want you and everyone else to know that you are," I add. Gesturing to Easton again, he rolls his eyes and pulls out the ring box from his pocket. Stella is still just standing inside the doorway, and I walk over to her, taking her hand in mine.

"Are you... are you asking me to marry you?" Stella looks between the two of us, and I guide her over to Easton.

"Legally, we both can't marry you, but we want you to know that we care about you enough to show our love for you to the world. We want everyone to know that you belong to us and that you're ours," I explain, and Easton pops the box open, revealing a three-stone diamond ring resembling our love story.

"I..." Stella swallows and tucks a strand of blonde hair behind her ear. "I'm just surprised... it's beautiful," she finally says.

"Is that a yes, no, or maybe?" Easton asks impatiently.

"Oh, my god, yes," she squeals, and I damn near sigh out loud.

"Let's see what it looks like on you." Easton takes the ring from the box and places it on Stella's already outstretched finger.

The ring slides on easily, and I admire how beautiful it looks on her. It screams mine and makes my beast, the part of me chained to her, howl at the moon. *Ours. Always and forever.* My cock starts to harden, but I push the sinful thoughts I'm having away.

"It's… it's heavy and big, so big." Her soft eyes widen as she looks up from the ring and at us.

"I can show you something else that's heavy and big." Easton wiggles his eyebrows and the sides of Stella's pink lips tilt up.

"Way to ruin the moment, dude." I want to smack Easton upside the head, but Stella just giggles.

"Can you now?" She lifts a brow, "Turns out after the day of classes I've had, I need to be shown how much my two men love me."

"What happened?" I question, worried I may have to kill someone. *Again.* Though James' death was never our fault.

"Let's not talk about that. I want you to do things to my body that will make me forget my name. Using your tongue," she takes a step forward and flicks the button on Easton's jeans, before moving onto mine. "And fingers." She licks her lips, "And the big and heavy things you were talking about, god, don't forget about those. One in my ass and one in my pussy."

She blushes as she says the dirty words. Even after a year of dirtying her up, she somehow kept a piece of her innocence in that.

"Who do you want in your ass?" I ask, my gaze sweeping over her body as she grabs the hem of her shirt and tugs if off and over her head.

"You, of course," she snickers and then hooks her thumbs into the sides of her yoga pants before shoving them down her legs. Reaching back, she undoes her bra and lets it fall to the floor with the rest of her clothes. Last, but not least, she dips her fingers into the waistband of her satin panties and shoves them down her legs impatiently. My tongue almost falls out of my mouth at the image of her before us. My mouth waters and the head of my cock peeks out of my jeans. Perks of going commando.

Creamy smooth skin, perky tits, and a flat stomach that leads to a land that I want to get lost in, that I want and need to worship a hundred times over.

Easton is an eager fucker and already has his pants and shirt off. I drag my gaze away from Stella's silky-smooth legs for one second to pull my shirt off. Then I shove my hands down over my thighs and kick them away once they reach my ankles.

Easton grabs Stella by the hips, pulling her into his chest. He kisses her with such force, she whimpers, but she's not whimpering with pain. No, our girl wants more, needs more from us.

"What do you want, baby? Sweet and gentle or hard and rough?"

"Everything..." She pants, crazed with need. "Yes, this is what I need right now... Everything. Hard, slow, gentle, rough. I need you both. However I can have you."

"We can arrange that," I'm the one smirking now. Lifting her off her feet, she lets out a gasp when I carry her to the bed and throw her onto the mattress.

Before her body stops bouncing, we are on her. Both of our mouths on her skin. All four of our hands all over her body, not leaving an inch of flesh untouched, unkissed, and unravished. She squirms beneath us like she is trying to get away, but her tiny hands are pulling us closer, her legs wrapping around us, anchoring us together.

Easton lays back on the bed and pulls Stella onto his lap. She mewls into the air as I come up behind her, my lips moving along her shoulders. I know the instant Easton's cock enters her because her entire body shivers, and the softest gasp I've ever heard slips from her lips. I suck on the tender flesh as he starts to fuck her, thrusting deep and hard.

Wrapping my hand into her hair, I tug her head back and snake an arm around her body, pinching one of her perky nipples.

She rides Easton's cock while her back is pressed against my chest, my cock caught between our bodies.

"How does it feel, baby? How does his huge cock feel inside your tight pussy?" I nip at her earlobe.

"Good, so good." She moans the words, and Easton starts to thrust faster and faster, the only thing keeping her body in place are my hands.

"Fall apart, Stella, fall, and we'll catch you just as we always do."

"Fuck, you're so tight, so perfect, so fucking mine," Easton roars. I release my hand on Stella's hair and force her to bend forward, giving me access to her puckered little asshole. Grabbing the lube from the nightstand, I pour a generous amount into my hand and stroke my cock in it.

Then I situate myself behind Stella, placing my hand against the small of her back.

"You want my cock in your ass?"

"Oh, yes, please... I need to come..." Stella cries out as Easton holds her in place with a steel grip. Guiding my cock to her ass, I see stars as I ease into the tight puckered hole, pure euphoric pleasure washes over me, and it's like I've died and gone to heaven.

"Shit, fuck, shit...."

"Fuck me," Stella pleads, and I do. Sinking balls deep inside her ass, I give her a moment before I start thrusting my hips, zings of intense pleasure zip up my spine.

"I'm coming... oh, god. I'm coming."

Like a rocket, Stella goes off, and there isn't any holding back our own releases. It doesn't take but a couple more strokes for Easton to explode inside her. As they both come down from their high, Stella resting her face against his sweaty chest, I up my pace, fucking her ass with deep hard thrusts.

"You want my come? You want me to fill your ass with my seed? You want to be my slut? Tell me now... tell me..." I order, my chest heaving. I'm on the edge of my release, and I need to hear her say it.

"Please. Please, fill my ass up with your come. Dirty me up, Cam... make me yours."

Rutting harder than I ever have before, I explode inside her, an animalistic roar escaping my lips and filling the room. Sweaty and completely spent, I pull out of her and sag to the spot beside Easton. Stella remains still for a long moment before she slides between our bodies, and like a missing puzzle piece, we come together, going from two to three.

"You're mine, and I'm yours," she whispers sleepily, her hand resting against my chest, the ring catching in the dim lighting, reminding me of the promise we made to her. Though marriage may never be able to happen for us, tonight we took our relationship to a level that will ensure everyone knows who she is to us, and who we are to her.

Forever. For always. Ours.

THE END.

NEXT IN THIS SERIES

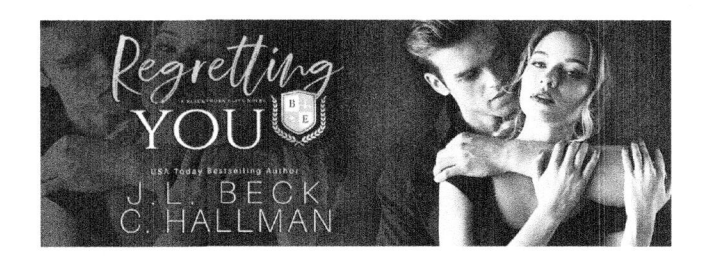

Regretting You

I'd never regretted knowing anyone like I did Kennedy Meyers.

Once upon a time she was my sister's best friend.

I'd always loved and wanted her to be mine, that is until the night everything changed and my love morphed into pure hatred.

Now I'm a vile bastard with a chip on his shoulder. Cruel black hate is all I know. My only focus *ucking my way through Blackthorn's elite women and partying.

Then she shows up. She's different now, quiet and reserved, but just as beautiful as she was the day she disappeared.

One look and my focus changes. I decided then that my time for revenge is now. No way does she get to enjoy herself. No, I'm going to make her life hell. Destroy her from the inside out.

I'm going to make her regret ever walking my way, because if it wasn't for her...my sister would still be alive.

Get it Now!

ABOUT THE AUTHORS

J.L. Beck and C. Hallman are an international bestselling author duo who write contemporary and dark romance.

Find all of our books, links, and signs on our website
www.bleedingheartromance.com

Beck and Hallman

BLEEDING HEART ROMANCE

- **f** CASSANDRAHALLMAN
  AUTHORJLBECK

- **Ⓞ** CASSANDRA_HALLMAN
  AUTHORJLBECK

- **BB** CASSANDRAHALLMAN
  JLBECK

ALSO BY THE AUTHORS

CONTEMPORAY ROMANCE

North Woods University
The Bet
The Dare
The Secret
The Vow
The Promise
The Jock

Bayshore Rivals
When Rivals Fall
When Rivals Lose
When Rivals Love

Breaking the Rules
Kissing & Telling
Babies & Promises
Roommates & Thieves

Also by the Authors

***

DARK ROMANCE

The Blackthorn Elite
Hating You
Breaking You
Hurting You
Regretting You

The Obsession Duet
Cruel Obsession
Deadly Obsession

The Rossi Crime Family
Convict Me
Protect Me
Keep Me
Guard Me
Tame Me
Remember Me

***

EROTIC STANDALONES

Runaway Bride

Their Captive

His Gift

Printed in Great Britain
by Amazon